# LEGACY OF BOIS

## Book 1 of The Boisdepin Chronicles

Justin Charles

Sando Savant Communications LLC

sando
savant
COMMUNICATIONS

To my cousin, Sharon. Thank you for believing in me when this story was nothing more than scattered ideas and stubborn dreams. For reading every chapter, every rewrite, and for enduring my passionate rants and endless excitement with patience and love. Your faith in me helped turn silence into story.

To my wife, Jasmine, and our children, Olivia and Caleb. Thank you for giving me the gift of time, for your quiet encouragement, and for letting me chase this lifelong dream even when it pulled me away for a while. Your love is the foundation beneath every word on these pages.

This book exists because of you.

# FOREWORD

I was born in Trinidad and Tobago, in a place where the air is always thick with stories. Stories in the rustle of bamboo, in the call of the Scarlet Ibis, in the rumble of thunder that rolls across the hills before the rain. I grew up hearing old people talk about the soucouyant and La Diablesse like they were neighbors. I saw moko jumbies walk the streets at Carnival and never once doubted they were guardians watching over us from above. Folklore was not a thing I read in books. It was in the dirt beneath my nails, in the songs on the breeze, in the fear and wonder we felt when night fell and the bush got quiet.

For almost two decades now, I have lived abroad. I have built a life elsewhere, far from the hummingbirds and poui trees. But Trinidad and Tobago never left me. It lingers in how I speak, how I dream, how I still measure time by rainy season and dry season. In foreign places, I carry it like a heartbeat I cannot silence. I miss the way the sun hits the Gulf of Paria at dusk. I miss the smell of chadon beni on my fingers. I miss the feeling of belonging to a land that holds both beauty and pain, history and hope.

This book is my love letter to that land. To our myths and our music, our spirits and our people. It is for the jumbies and the douens, for Papa Bois and Mama D'leau, for every whisper of the forest that says we were here long before concrete and glass tried to silence us. It is for those of us who left and still feel the island tugging behind our ribs. And for those who stayed and kept the old stories alive.

Writing this story has been an act of memory and healing. It is my way of honoring the place that shaped me, even when I could not be there to walk its roads. It is also a promise to my younger self, the child who wrote worlds in the margins of schoolbooks and believed that our stories were just as magical, just as worthy, as anything written in faraway lands.

If you are from Trinidad and Tobago, I hope you see pieces of home in these pages. If you are not, I hope you leave with a little more wonder and a little more respect for this small place that holds so much soul.

Thank you for opening this book. Thank you for giving my homeland room to breathe inside your imagination.

I truly hope you enjoy it.

— Justin Charles

# TABLE OF CONTENTS

# CHAPTER 1 - ATIBA

The elk was majestic.

Was it an elk? Atiba actually didn't know what an elk looked like for certain. A male deer, maybe? A moose? No, definitely not a moose. Probably a male deer. Whatever it was, his encounter with the animal had left quite the impression on the young man. It wasn't so much how beautiful he thought the creature was, as it was WHERE he'd seen it.

The quaint rural seaside Trinidadian village of Boisdepin (Bwah-deh-pon) was flanked by bushy forests and the sprawling Caribbean Sea, so it wasn't uncommon to encounter the occasional wild animal. But Atiba hadn't seen the animal on a leisurely jaunt through the village.

It had appeared before him in a church, filled to the brim with mourners, during his grandfather's funeral service.

It appeared out of thin air, during the preacher's impassioned sermon, sauntered up to the casket with an otherworldly grace, and laid its head low to touch its longhorns to the body that rested within. There was a hint of reverence in the act, as though this elk/deer thing was doing what came naturally at a funeral, paying its respects.

The sheer absurdity of the scene, as it occurred, had left Atiba stunned, especially since no one else in the small church sanctuary even acknowledged the animal's existence. By the time he'd recovered, the animal had turned to fix its austere gaze on him. Fear kept the young man rooted to the spot, and the world around them seemed to fall away as it slowly approached where he sat in the front pew. It stopped just a few feet away from him, and then bowed its horned head once again, as though inviting Atiba to touch it. Despite his apprehension, a strange feeling told him that it was safe to do so.

He gingerly reached out and let his fingers graze the animal's sturdy, rough horns, tracing the length of its pattern in an almost affectionate manner.

And then, just like that, it vanished. The world came back into focus, and the funeral continued unimpeded.

The incident had taken up a little over a minute of the two days he'd been in Trinidad thus far, but he couldn't stop thinking about it. Was the strange animal's appearance linked to the infamous "Day of Darkness" that befell Trinidad seven years ago?

The "Day of Darkness" moniker made the incident seem more ominous than it actually was. As Atiba understood it, and from the many videos taken that day he'd seen on social media, the sky across the island suddenly became as black as night, as though a switch had been flipped, and then, after ten minutes, just as suddenly, it became light again.

Scientists from around the world scrambled to try to explain the phenomenon. It hadn't been a solar eclipse, since the sun, though muted in color and as dark as the rest of the sky, was still directly visible. Try as they might, no one could figure out why it had happened. However, even though the cause was unknown, its long-term effects soon became apparent.

People all over Trinidad began to report sightings of, and encounters with creatures embedded within the island's folklore; and in such numbers that it became a key topic of conversation among news outlets and the citizenry alike. Of course, there was never any proof. Given the prevalence of social media, zero videos and zero pictures of the purported encounters relegated such sightings to mere hoaxes. But now he'd had an encounter of his own.

Atiba had been born in Trinidad, but raised in the United States and, as such, had no connection to Trinidad's culture beyond his mother's thick accent and the cuisine she often cooked. In general, he had never been one to believe in superstition, the occult, or anything of that sort. Still, the moment the automatic doors that separated the Piarco International Airport and the rest of Trinidad slid open, and the blast of warm, fresh Caribbean air buffeted his face, he couldn't help but feel that there was something magical about the island.

He had come specifically because of the death of his grandfather, Wilberforce DuBois. He hadn't even WANTED to come. Even though he'd spent the first five years of his life under the man's care, Atiba couldn't recall much about that time, nor Wilberforce himself. He didn't know the man, so why did he have to come to his funeral, to Trinidad?

His mother, Wilberforce's estranged firstborn, held the firm belief that the man would leave him an inheritance, despite their own tempestuous relationship. Even more importantly, she had given Atiba explicit instructions to contest any other result.

His grandfather had had another daughter and she and her son were still in the picture and were apparently very close to the old man. An aunt and cousin he'd never met before today. They seemed like nice enough people, but he couldn't help but feel awkward around them.

Of course, he'd never intended on disputing his grandfather's will. Whatever the beef had been between his mother and Wilberforce was theirs and theirs alone. After all, if she couldn't be bothered to attend her own father's funeral, why should she or her offspring benefit?

Surprisingly, though, he hadn't needed to. His grandfather wasn't an especially wealthy man, but he had left Atiba his most important possessions: a modest amount of cash, the well-maintained, colonial-era, wooden fret-worked ginger-bread style house that sat atop a hill overlooking the rest of the village, and third, an old wooden bangle.

Atiba had no way of knowing exactly how old it was, but ancient seemed to be the correct descriptor. The bangle was made of plain, lacquered, sand-colored wood with no distinctive markings to speak of. It gave off an interesting odor, an earthy scent mixed with a tiny bit of that geriatric smell you'd probably find at a nursing home. He didn't know exactly why his grandfather had left him such a personal item, but he found himself liking it. If it had been the only thing he'd received from this trip to Trinidad, he'd have been satisfied.

Sitting on the stoop of his grandfather's… well, now his home… after the day's events, Atiba stretched his hand out and gazed admiringly at it as it hung from his wrist. The entire village had shown up at the house for the repast, and the revelry was still going strong. Atiba, though, had abandoned it. He didn't belong here.

"Hey."

Snapping out of his reverie, he glanced up to see his cousin, hand outstretched, offering him a chilled Carib beer. Atiba hesitated for a second, slightly taken aback by this kind gesture from someone who was essentially a stranger to him. A stranger who'd just stolen his inheritance to boot.

His cousin was what the locals called a 'dougla', a person of mixed African and East Indian heritage, and looked to be around Atiba's own age, 20 or 21. He had a thin frame, but the toned forearms jutting from his rolled-up shirtsleeves hinted at an athletic build. His hair was a unique mix between spiky and tousled, obviously kept in place with way too much hair product. And then there were his eyes: golden, bright and unblinking, catching the light in a way that seemed almost unnatural. For all the flash of his style, the grin he wore was warm and genuine, and Atiba found himself disarmed despite the rest.

"Hey," Atiba replied, accepting the bottle and taking a huge gulp.

His cousin's smile widened, taking the act as an invitation to drop onto the stoop beside him. "De name's Prakesh," he said, lifting his own beer in a casual salute. "Call me Prak, doh. Everyone does."

Atiba managed a small, bashful smile and nodded. "Atiba. Good to meet you, Prak."

For a while, the two sat in companionable silence, nursing their beers, eyes drifting out over the village that spread below their grandfather's house.

"Look, Prak… I'm sorry about—"

"Nah, man," Prak cut in with an easy chuckle. "None ah dat. We is family."

Atiba shook his head quickly. "Y'all were so much closer to him though. I don't deserve his generosity. I don't even… remember him."

"Ay, you doh worry 'bout me and moms," Prak said, shrugging. "Grandpa made sure we good. And you might not remember him, but trust me, he remember you."

Atiba blinked. "He did?"

"Yeah, boss." Prak grinned, though it softened into a grimace. "When it come to he grandchirren, Wilberforce could talk yuh ears off. Especially 'bout he grandson in the States." He shook his head with a laugh. "It was actually realllll embarrassin' sometimes."

The levity in his tone cracked the last of the tension, and both young men laughed, the sound carrying easy into the night.

"What was he like? I mean… can you tell me about him?"

Prak tapped his chin, his eyes drifting as though pulling memories from the air.

"Well… he was a realllll serious fella. Stric' an' no-nonsense, but very fair-minded. He was de kinda man who woulda' gih yuh de shirt off he back if he thought yuh needed it more. Dat's why everybody in de village loves—"

He stumbled, the brightness in his voice dimming for a beat.

"…loved him, I mean. He help all a' dem one time or another."

"Sounds like a good man." Atiba sighed, lifting his wrist. The wooden bangle caught the porch light, smooth from years of wear. He stared hard at it, willing it to open some buried door in his mind. But nothing came.

No scent, no voice, no half-formed memory. Just blank space where those years should have been. Like whole pages torn from a book. The frustration curdled in his chest, and he let out a low growl, drowning it with another swig of beer.

Prak caught the shift in his cousin's face. His golden eyes softened, catching the light as he leaned in with a grin meant to cut through the heaviness. "How long yuh in Trinidad for?"

Atiba hesitated. His ticket said a week. But when he really thought about it, there wasn't much waiting for him back home. Just a shaky job market and the slow choke of student loan debt. "I've got a couple days left," he said finally. He lifted a brow. "What'd you have in mind?"

"Ah doh know if yuh know, but is Carnival time now," Prak said, his golden eyes lighting up. "Leh we go party, man. Ah go show yuh how we does do it here in Trinidad."

Atiba couldn't help grinning at his cousin's excitement, but he shook his head. He drank now and then with friends, sure, but he was no party person. Never had been. Crowds, noise, wild energy… none of it was his scene. He was more at home with a book in hand or an Xbox controller under his thumbs, in between endless job searches. "Sorry, bro, I'm—"

The sudden buzz in his pocket cut him short. Fishing out his phone, he gave Prak a quick nod, a silent hold that thought, before answering.

"'Tiba, what he leave yuh?"

Atiba blinked, phone pressed to his ear. "Hey to you too, Mom."

"Boy, doh play wit meh, eh?" Her voice was clipped, all business. "What he leave yuh?"

His lip curled as he bit down hard, trying to keep the disgust from spilling out. Her father's body wasn't even a day in the ground, and this was all she had to say. He steadied himself before she could repeat the question.

"The house in Boisdepin. The land around it. And… a lot of money."

"TANK YOU JESUS!"

The shriek nearly blew out the receiver, but Atiba had the foresight to hold the phone at arm's length.

Then her tone snapped back to business.

"Nobody eh fight yuh for it?"

Atiba cast a quick glance at Prak, lowering his voice. "No, Mom."

"Good!" Just like that, her cheer returned. "Dah money goin' straight to meh business."

Her business. Atiba almost laughed, but it came out as a scoff under his breath. That so-called 'business' was nothing more than a pyramid scheme she refused to admit had bled her dry. Every dollar he scraped together from odd jobs back home had vanished into it.

He hadn't wanted Wilberforce's money if it meant robbing others who deserved it more. But after Prak's reassurance… maybe he could finally put it to use himself.

"Mom," he said hesitantly, "The lawyer said it could take up to a year before I even have access to the money or for the house to be transferred to me." He gulped. "When the money comes… I was planning to use it to pay off my student loans."

Predictably, that proclamation did not go well. "Who de hell yuh tink yuh talkin' to, eh!?"

Atiba didn't even flinch. He was too used to her eruptions, too conditioned by years of shouting matches that always ended the same way. For a split second he thought about trying again, pushing back… but the weight of all those failed attempts pressed down. He sighed. "Sorry, Mom."

"Ah doh want to hear no more foolishness from you," she snapped, steamrolling over his apology. Then, almost grudgingly, she added, "Fine. If yuh have to wait, yuh have to wait. Buh when de time come, yuh goin' back and sort it out."

"Yes, Mom."

"Good." Her tone finally softened, satisfied at having bent him back into shape. And then she hung up.

Atiba stared at his phone in impotent frustration, gripping it so tightly that his knuckles grew pale.

"Offer still stands," Prak said, pushing himself up and giving Atiba a sympathetic look.

Other than that loud outburst, Atiba was sure his cousin hadn't caught the details of what his mother had planned for their grandfather's estate. Still, he must've been giving off some major depressing vibes.

He looked up at Prak and, for the first time, really saw him—not just the bright smile, the easy banter, or the golden eyes that always seemed to carry a joke. No, beneath it all, Prak was someone who seemed… content.

Genuinely happy with his lot in life.

A flicker of envy stirred in Atiba's chest, sharp and undeniable. But layered with it was something quieter, steadier—hope. Maybe being close to Wilberforce, to Boisdepin itself, gave Prak that groundedness. Maybe, if he let it, it could take root in him too.

"Y'know what, Prak," he said, standing up as well, "Screw it. Let's go party."

"Bro." His cousin's eyes lit up mischievously. "Welcome to Trinidad."

# CHAPTER 2 - ESME

he short, gasping bursts of wind that hammered against the shutters were accompanied by low, whistling groans. Combined with the rustling of countless leaves and the pitter-patter of raindrops assaulting the earth, the sound seemed to mirror the foreboding nature of the raven-shrouded night sky upon which it rode. The full moon was obscured by large storm clouds, though there were areas where patches of moonlight were able to penetrate. It was one of these patches that made its way onto the floor of Duncan Morris' tiny bedroom.

Duncan was what many would consider an ugly man. Droopy, recessed eyes were nestled under unnaturally thick brows. These features gave way to sunken cheeks, a beak-like nose, and a square jaw. Overall, his face had all the visual pleasantries as those of an orangutan. His only aesthetic saving grace was his lean, well-sculpted figure; a boon which he exploited at every turn. At every physically intensive activity, he excelled. He was an accomplished sportsman, mixed martial artist, thug for hire, domestic abuser...

...and it was the latter that had brought him into his current predicament.

Spared from the chaos of the storm outside, save for the occasional droplet that had breached the ceiling to splatter onto the floor, Duncan was far from safe. He stood precariously on a rickety wooden stool, his arms pulled tight behind his back and bound with garroting wire. Around his neck, a noose stretched upward, tethering him to the rafters. The coarse rope bit into his skin, making each shallow breath a battle.

Sweat dripped down his forehead, trailing across his weathered features as the stool wobbled beneath him. His breathing was fast, erratic, his bloodshot eyes fixed with fury on a single orange dot flickering in the darkness just beyond the moonlit patch of floor ahead of him.

"Yuh dead! Ah go kill yuh!" Duncan growled, his voice hoarse and strained. The stool shifted dangerously beneath his weight, creaking in protest.

From the shadows, a faint wisp of smoke curled into the air, followed by a soft exhalation. The voice that responded was calm, almost mocking. "Is that right?" The words carried an unnerving confidence. "I'm not the one hanging from the rafters."

Duncan snarled. "Take meh dong, yuh little piss—!" His words were cut short as a lit cigarette came sailing from the darkness, hitting him square in the mouth. He gagged, coughing violently as the cigarette tumbled to the floor. His angry spitting and cursing filled the small room, but his tormentor paid it no mind.

The figure stepped forward, emerging into the faint moonlight. Duncan's furious expression froze, his blood running cold.

What stood before him was no ordinary person. The figure's body seemed to be made entirely of shadows, but not shadows in the sense of obscurity or concealment. This was something else—something otherworldly. The figure's form was solid yet shifting, a humanoid mass of swirling purple-black darkness. Faint patterns glimmered within its surface:

nebulae swirling lazily, constellations winking in and out of existence, as if the night sky had come to life.

"What… what de hell is dat? Who you is!?" Duncan's voice cracked, his bravado replaced by raw terror.

The figure tilted its head, an eerily human gesture that somehow felt predatory. Its voice resonated like an echo within a cavern. "Who or what I am isn't important." It took another step forward, the cosmic patterns within its form shifting hypnotically. "But you… you're the guest of honor."

Duncan's chest heaved as he struggled against his bindings, his face a mix of anger and fear. "Wha yuh want wit' me?"

The shadowy figure's outline rippled, its nebulous surface seeming to shiver. It leaned closer, the suggestion of a face hovering mere inches from Duncan's own. "A little birdie told me you like to put your hands on women. Hurt them. Control them." Its tone sharpened, cold and cutting as a blade. "That ends now."

"What I want, Duncan dear, is to just issue a friendly little warning. Do you know how long it takes for a man to bleed out if his testicles are cut off?" it whispered, chuckling a bit at Duncan's startled reaction. "Mess around, lay a finger on yuh wife again, and yuh go find out."

In a flash, its leg whipped forward and the stool that Duncan was perched upon went sailing towards the corner of the room. Duncan's neck stretched as gravity pulled the rope taut around it. His face grew beet red and his eyes bulged as his legs kicked out in a vain search for solid footing.

The figure stared up at the struggling man for a moment, seemingly immune to the short, stuttering gasps as its captive flailed around. When it was sure its message had been effectively received, it grabbed the stool.

Taking its time, the figure reached up with a knife it produced from seemingly nowhere and cut the rope, causing Duncan to crumple to the floor, unceremoniously.

Hopping back down again and kneeling beside him, the figure patted his cheek playfully. "I advise you not to mess around, Mr. Morris," it said, ignoring his violent, hacking coughs as he swallowed huge breaths of air, "...and trust me, I'll know if you do."

Before Duncan could muster a reply, the figure's form began to shift. Slowly, the swirling shadows peeled away, like smoke caught in an invisible breeze. The darkness receded, unraveling to reveal what lay beneath: a young man.

He appeared to be in his early twenties, his light brown skin, pale and sickly-looking, stark against the dim light. His short, cropped hair clung to his damp forehead, and his wide, unseeing eyes were filled with fear. He stood motionless for a heartbeat before his body crumpled to the floor, unconscious.

The shadows did not vanish. They continued to retreat, flowing along the walls and floor like a living tide, spilling out of the windows into the storm. They slithered across the drenched exterior of the house, climbing walls and darting between cracks until they coalesced at the feet of a woman leaning casually against the wall outside.

She stood an even five feet tall, her dark chocolate skin shimmering as rain slicked her full, yet athletic frame. Her wild black hair shot out from beneath a bright yellow bandana, framing her face in erratic curls. Almond-shaped eyes glinted with quiet intensity, and her black t-shirt and fitted jeans clung to her curves. She was young, but the perpetual scowl etched into her features spoke of hard-fought battles and sleepless nights.

The shadows pooled around her feet before vanishing entirely into the stormy night. She pushed herself off the wall, her lips curving into a dangerous smile.

Inside, Duncan lay sprawled on the floor, coughing and gasping for air, his mind reeling. The unconscious young man beside him was a puzzle he couldn't begin to solve.

A thrall. A newly secured, random asset she'd chosen to play the role of villain.

There would be nothing to link this back to her or to her friend, the object of Duncan's abuse, Minnie.

Outside, the woman turned on her heel and strode into the rain. Her job here was done.

Dougie's Bar wasn't the most fancy place around. It took up the first floor of a nondescript, wooden two-story building in the middle of a mostly residential area.

Every morning at 8 am, like clockwork, the titular Dougie would descend from his home on the second floor and open up shop. And as he had for the past few months, he found Esme Walcott propped up against the front door of the establishment, waiting.

"Yuh late," she muttered.

Dougie sighed. "You early," he retorted, fidgeting with his keys.

Once inside, the young woman took up her usual seat at the bar and waited patiently as Dougie went about his usual morning routine. Once he was finally back behind the bar, she gave him a sweet look, drumming her fingers on the counter in front of her expectantly. The man sighed and went to work, soon presenting the woman with a rum and coke. She gave him another childish grin and winked as she downed the drink in one gulp.

"You doh have any other place to be, miss lady?" Dougie asked, incredulously, as he presented her with another glass, "Like work?"

He had to wait for her to finish downing the new glass before he got a reply. "I eh tell yuh? I get fired."

Dougie arched an eyebrow. "If I remember correctly, yuh had yuh own psychology practice."

"Ah fire mihself," Esme shrugged, "Another rum and coke. Leave de bottle dis time."

The man simply sighed once more and did as asked. Esme had been just an occasional customer back in the day, always exceptionally dressed and well-spoken but she'd suddenly stopped coming around. He had no idea what had happened to her during her absence, but when she suddenly showed up that morning months ago, she was completely different. He couldn't help thinking that she was wasting her life away, but he didn't actively discourage her. She was always respectful toward him, always paid her tab, got along fine with his other regulars, and didn't cause trouble aside from kicking out anyone who got too fresh with her.

The sudden audio sting of a breaking news report caught his attention and he peered up at the TV that overlooked the bar.

"Breaking news: a young mother of three has been murdered in San Fernando," the announcer stated in the typical newsman flare, "Minnie DeVerteil's body was found by her mother, strangled to death in her bedroom."

Dougie set to washing Esme's first glass, shaking his head in pity as the news report continued. Crime and violence against women in Trinidad had unfortunately always been a thing, but these days it seemed to be becoming much more prevalent. Almost as frequent as the purported sightings of jumbies and the like since "The Day of Darkness".

"No!!!!!"

The sudden sound of shattering glass, followed by a loud, mournful wail made Dougie nearly jump out of his skin. He wheeled around to face the bar and was met by a sight that made his blood run cold.

Esme's face was contorted into a tortured mixture of intense grief and unfathomable rage. Tears streamed down her face from bloodshot eyes and pinpoint pupils. Her fists were clenched tightly on the counter, blood pooling around her left hand, mixing with the remnants of her drink and shards of broken glass.

"Ah go kill him!!!"

Dougie gasped as a slight frost began to envelop the counter, spreading outwards from where the woman's fists lay, and growing in intensity until its surface was completely covered in a rough, icy sheen.

"Ah go kill him!!!!"

He had absolutely no idea what was going on, but he had a feeling that bringing Esme's attention to him at this point would not end well for him.

"Ah go kill him!!!!!!!!!!"

Dougie didn't know exactly who the "him" she referenced was, but he instinctively knew she meant it.

"The victim's common-law husband, Duncan Morris, believed to Ms. DeVerteil's killer was later found dead in a separate apartment. Police believe that he took his own life, making this a case of apparent murder-suicide."

The look of utter shock and disbelief on Esme's face stood in stark contrast to her earlier expression. The tears continued in full force as the young woman lay her head on her arms on the cold, ice-covered counter and bawled her heart out. Dougie wasn't at all an emotional man, but his heart ached with each wretched sob that escaped her lips.

Esme and this woman must've been close.

As confused as he was about what could have possibly caused the ice, he pushed that thought aside for the moment and did what came naturally to him. After a few seconds of preparation, he sat another full glass of rum and coke next to her and turned his attention back to something… anything that wasn't the crying woman.

Eventually, the sobs quieted, and the sound of ice tinkling against glass let him know it was safe to turn around. The glass was empty. Esme glanced up at him, looking completely dejected, despondent even. Allowing herself one more sniffle, she rose to her feet, grabbed the bottle of rum he'd left earlier, and moved unsteadily to a table at the back of the room.

# CHAPTER 3 - ATIBA

The journey to the village of Boisdepin from the main highway consisted of a single, expansive stretch of coastal road that hugged the sharp curves and the occasional treacherous hairpin turns of the steep, tree-covered hill-side, the surface of which was so uneven and jagged that it had garnered quite the reputation among the locals for resembling a cheese-grater in appearance.

On the other side of the road, beyond the shockingly yellow and white-striped guard rails, and about a hundred feet below, the ocean spread forth for miles, colliding with the distant sky. At sunrise, an unearthly hue, a fiery mixture of crimson and orange blanketed the sky, seemingly being swallowed up by the sea. The resulting phenomenon made it almost impossible to tell where they intersected, the horizon being swallowed up by the dawn.

Such a sight would be sure to captivate any who saw it; nonetheless, Atiba paid it no mind. A miracle of nature such as the view now rushing past him didn't really matter when you were seconds away from throwing up.

The last two days had been a whirlwind for the cousins and Atiba had added a lot of local words to his vocabulary. The parties, what the locals called fetes, were all high-energy, loud, and wild affairs. Being packed amidst the throngs of people grinding and "wining" their hips, dancing passionately, provocatively, and energetically to soca music was the most exhilarating experience of Atiba's life. He had been to many nightclubs back home, mostly as a designated driver for his friends, but never had he been so drawn to take part in the revelry.

Every night, he and Prak would make the trip from the little village to various, often far-flung, party destinations around Trinidad. For the past 24 hours, Prak had increased the intensity of their fete experience. It was one party after another, culminating in an all-night bash on Maracas beach.

Atiba had never gotten so drunk in his entire life. And now, as the two made their way back home, came the obligatory hangover.

Atiba's stomach churned violently and he let out a simpering groan as he lay prone in the back seat of Prak's modest Mitsubishi Lancer and tried his best to delay the inevitable. His cousin, at the wheel, flashed him an impish grin via the rearview mirror.

"Boss… Ent ah tell yuh to pace yuhself? But noooo~!" he quipped, playfully, and then continued in a mock American accent, "Man, worry about yourself, I can handle me."

Atiba groaned again and avoided his cousin's gaze, ashamed that he'd let himself get this wasted. As the car drew closer to the village, the surrounding rocky cliffs gave way to bushy forests on either side and by then, the young man knew he'd reached his limit.

"Pull over!"

The car screeched to a halt on the side of the road, and Atiba spilled out into the early dawn. He lurched forward onto the grass on his hands and knees and threw up so hard that tears spilled from his eyes. Then a second time, then a third, then a fourth, until finally, he managed to get himself under control. He took a few deep breaths, doing his best to ignore the smell of his vomit, and lamented how this inability to hold his alcohol must look to Prak. Taking one more deep breath, he raised his head and nearly had a heart attack when he came face to face with a child.

"Oh crap!!!" Atiba scrambled backward in surprise until he sat with his back against the car, all the while never taking his eyes off of the kid.

The child was skinny and stood about three feet tall, with bronze-colored skin. He couldn't tell whether it was a boy or a girl. A few rags covered its midsection, and a large, dome-shaped straw hat hid its eyes and nose. Its small O-shaped mouth and somewhat comical pot-belly were its most distinguishing features.

Not the thing one expected to find on the side of the road in the middle of nowhere.

The child tilted its head, then crouched to pick up something on the ground in front of it. Atiba's eyes widened when he saw what it was. A cell phone. HIS cell phone. It must've fallen out of his pocket when he stumbled out of the car. It turned the phone over in its tiny hands, observing it for a while, and then with a mischievous grin, took off into the forest.

"Hey!" he yelled out, hopping onto his feet, "Give that back!"

He took a few running steps as he started to give chase, but then he stopped himself. He was exhausted, he was hungry, he felt sick and he was in no mood to run after some local kid into a dark forest. He could always get another cell phone. He took one last look into the thick brush and, finding no sign of the child, hopped back into the car.

"Feel better?" asked Prak, pulling off.

"Yeah, I guess," he answered. "Hey, can I borrow your phone for a sec? Need to send a message to my mom real quick."

"Sure." His cousin tossed it to him over his shoulder.

"Wha' happen' to yours? Loss' track of it at a party or wah?"

Atiba shook his head as he used his cousin's phone to access his email and send his mother a quick heads-up that his own phone had been lost. "Nah, it fell out of my pocket when I was throwing up just now and some kid bolted with it."

"A kid? Just now?" The confused tone in Prak's voice made Atiba doubly certain that this was a strange occurrence. He'd had no clue if it was customary for people in rural Trinidad to allow their kids out of the house before the sun had even fully risen.

"Yeah, it was weird." Atiba replied, "I wasn't really paying attention so it would have been easy for the kid to sneak up on me, but…"

"But?"

"But it seemed like it just showed up out of thin air," he finished, shrugging.

"Hmm, wha' de chile look like?"

By the time Atiba finished describing the strange child, Prak's signature happy-go-lucky expression had darkened. Through the rearview mirror, he could see his cousin's eyes narrow. "Uh… what's up, Prak? You know the kid?"

Prak didn't respond, seemingly caught up in his own thoughts. "Prak?"

"Oh! Uh…" his cousin started, smiling apologetically, "Yeah, I guess yuh could say dat. Not well enough to get yuh phone back though. We go get yuh a new one. Oh, and…" He gave Atiba a serious look through the rearview mirror. "Could you not mention dat chile to anybody?"

"Uh… sure…"

"Thanks."

An uncomfortable silence hung over them for the rest of the ride. It was clear to Atiba that his encounter with the child had troubled Prak, but why?

The car rolled slowly through the narrow streets of Boisdepin, the village stirring to life as the first rays of sunlight spilled over the horizon. The air was thick with the salty tang of the sea, mingling with the earthy scent of dew-damp grass and the faint aroma of wood smoke curling from chimneys. Prak's Mitsubishi Lancer bumped gently over the uneven road, the tires crunching against the gravel as they passed rows of modest wooden houses, their brightly painted shutters thrown open to welcome the morning.

Atiba leaned his head against the window, his hangover still throbbing faintly behind his temples, but the nausea had subsided. He watched as the village unfolded before him, a patchwork of simple, everyday scenes that felt both foreign and strangely comforting. A rooster strutted across the road, its chest puffed out proudly as it let out a loud, piercing crow that echoed through the quiet streets. Chickens pecked at the ground nearby, their feathers ruffled and speckled with dirt, while a stray dog trotted lazily past, its tail wagging as it sniffed at the air. The smell of kerosene drifted from a neighbor's lamp that hadn't yet been put out. Sweet guava leaves, bruised underfoot, lent a faint tang. From somewhere farther off came the savory pull of smoked herring frying, laced with the sharper bite of onions. The dog's nose twitched, pulling the story of the village from the air.

Further down the road, a group of fishermen gathered on the beach, their voices carrying on the breeze as they hauled nets and prepared their boats for the day's catch. The sea sparkled in the early light, its surface rippling like liquid silver as it stretched out to meet the sky. Atiba could hear the rhythmic slap of waves against the shore, a soothing counterpoint to the distant chatter of the fishermen.

The village itself was a picture of quaint simplicity. The houses were small but well-kept, their wooden walls weathered to a soft gray by years of sun and salt. Brightly colored flowers spilled from window boxes and climbed trellises, their petals glistening with dew. Here and there, clotheslines stretched between houses, laden with laundry that fluttered gently in the breeze. The streets were lined with coconut palms, their fronds swaying lazily overhead, casting dappled shadows on the ground below.

As they climbed higher into the village, the road grew steeper, winding its way up the hillside until they reached a small, secluded house perched at the very top. It was a modest structure, its wooden fretwork and gingerbread trim giving it a distinctly colonial-era charm. The house was painted a soft, faded yellow, with white shutters and a red tin roof that gleamed in the morning light. A wide veranda wrapped around the front, offering a sweeping view of the village and the sea beyond.

Prak pulled the car to a stop in front of the house and turned to Atiba with a sheepish grin. "Ah forget someting back in town," he said, scratching the back of his head. "Ah go be back in a lil' bit, eh?"

Atiba raised an eyebrow, puzzled by his cousin's sudden departure. "You're leaving?"

"Yeah, yeah, it eh go take long," Prak assured him, already shifting the car into reverse. "Jus' make yuhself at home. Is your house now, right?"

Before Atiba could respond, Prak was already backing down the driveway, the tires kicking up a small cloud of dust as he sped off in the direction of the village. Atiba watched him go, a faint sense of unease settling in his chest. In all the time he'd spent with his cousin recently, it wasn't like Prak to be so abrupt, but he shrugged it off, attributing it to his cousin's usual eccentricities.

Turning back to the house, Atiba took a deep breath and climbed the steps to the veranda. The wooden planks creaked softly under his weight, and he paused for a moment to take in the view. From here, he could see the entire village spread out below, the rooftops glinting in the sunlight and the sea stretching out to the horizon. It was a peaceful, almost idyllic scene, and for a moment, he felt a strange sense of belonging.

He pushed open the front door and stepped inside, the hinges squeaking softly as it swung shut behind him. The interior of the house was small but cozy, with polished wooden floors and walls painted a soft, creamy white. The furniture was simple and functional, with a few pieces that looked like they had been handcrafted: a sturdy wooden table, a pair of rocking chairs, a bookshelf filled with well-worn volumes. The decor was sparse but tasteful, with a few framed photographs and small trinkets scattered here and there, giving the space a lived-in, nostalgic feel.

Atiba wandered through the house, his footsteps echoing softly in the quiet. The living room was dominated by a large, overstuffed armchair that looked like it had seen better days, its fabric faded and worn but still comfortable. A small side table sat next to it, holding a stack of books and a pair of reading glasses. Atiba ran his fingers over the spines of the books, noting titles on everything from Caribbean history to botany to folklore. His grandfather had clearly been a man of many interests.

The kitchen was small but tidy, with a cast-iron stove and a wooden countertop that had been scrubbed to a smooth, glossy finish. A row of mason jars lined the windowsill, filled with dried herbs and spices, their earthy scents mingling with the faint aroma of wood smoke that still lingered in the air. Atiba opened the refrigerator, half-expecting it to be empty, but it was stocked with fresh produce: bananas, mangoes, and a few containers of leftovers that smelled faintly of curry and spices.

He made his way back to the living room, his eyes drawn to a wall covered in framed photographs. He stepped closer, studying the images one by one. There were pictures of Wilberforce with various villagers: helping to repair a roof, standing proudly with a group of fishermen, playing cricket with a group of young men. In each photo, his grandfather looked stern but kind, his strong, weathered face set in a serious expression that somehow conveyed both authority and compassion.

One photo caught his eye, a group of children, their faces bright with laughter, clustered around Wilberforce. The old man stood tall and stoic in the center, his hands resting on the shoulders of two of the children, but there was a softness in his eyes that Atiba hadn't noticed before. The children seemed completely at ease with him, their smiles genuine and unguarded.

And then he saw it, a photo of himself. He was just a toddler, no more than three or four years old, sitting on Wilberforce's lap. The old man's face was as stern as ever, but there was a hint of a smile playing at the corners of his mouth. Atiba, on the other hand, was beaming, his chubby cheeks dimpled and his eyes crinkled with laughter. It was the only photo in which Wilberforce seemed even remotely happy.

Atiba stared at the photo, a strange ache settling in his chest. He couldn't remember this moment, or any moment from his early childhood. It was as though those years had been erased from his memory, leaving behind only a vague, unsettling void. What had his life been like back then? What kind of man had Wilberforce been to him? Why couldn't he remember?

He reached out and touched the edge of the frame, his fingers trembling slightly. He felt an aching sense of loss, sudden and deep, not just for the grandfather he had never known, but for the childhood he couldn't remember.

The house was quiet, the only sound the faint rustling of the curtains in the breeze. Atiba stood there for a long time, staring at the photo, lost in thought. Somewhere in the back of his mind, a question began to form— one that he knew he wouldn't be able to ignore for long.

What had happened during those first five years of his life? And why couldn't he remember?

Atiba's gaze lingered on the photo of himself and Wilberforce for a few more moments, then another set of photographs pulled him out of his thoughts. These were group photos, clearly taken years apart, and they told a story of their own.

The first was a picture of three youths. Prak, unmistakably in an unfortunate awkward pre-teen phase, stood in the middle, flanked by two older boys. Atiba couldn't help but chuckle at the sight of his cousin back then. Prak's frame was even skinnier than it was now, his hair cut into a bowl shape that did him no favors. His sheepish, shy grin was a far cry from the confident, charming personality he exuded today. The teenager on Prak's left had an expression of confidence and amiability that reminded Atiba of Prak's current demeanor. He was tall, with a simple crew cut and a relaxed posture, his light bronze skin glowing in the sunlight. The teen on Prak's right, however, was a stark contrast. He had his arms crossed and was looking away from the camera, his face a mask of surly annoyance. His curly black hair was a tangled mess, and his light bronze skin seemed to radiate defiance. Everything about him screamed that he didn't want to be there.

Atiba studied the photo, trying to piece together the dynamics between the three. Prak seemed at ease around the older boys, that much was clear, but the surly one's attitude was hard to ignore. Who were they? Friends?

Family? And where were they now?

The next photo appeared to have been taken three or four years later, judging by how much older Prak looked. In this one, Wilberforce stood in his usual stoic manner, watching Prak and the surly teen—now possibly an adult—engage in what looked like stick fighting. Both Prak and the surly one held sticks about an inch in diameter and four feet long, their bodies tense as they faced off against each other. The surly teen's hair had changed, now styled into a fauxhawk with a tail tied up in the back, but his expression was just as intense as ever. The smiling teen from the previous photo was absent, leaving Atiba to wonder what had happened to him.

Maybe he was the one taking the photo? The scene appeared to have taken place in the front yard of this very house, the familiar wooden fretwork of the veranda visible in the background.

The final photo of the set was simpler, just Wilberforce and Prak, seemingly taken not long before their grandfather's death. Prak looked as old as he did today, but there was a sadness in his eyes that even his smile couldn't hide. Atiba stared at the photo, his chest tightening. Prak had clearly been close to Wilberforce, closer than Atiba had ever been. What had their relationship been like? What had Wilberforce been like in his final years? And why did Prak seem so sad, even as he smiled for the camera?

As Atiba's gaze drifted from frame to frame, he was soon struck by what he didn't see.

There were no photographs of his mother.

He stepped closer to the wall, his fingers brushing against the edges of the frames as if hoping to uncover something hidden. But no matter how many times he looked, the absence was undeniable. Wilberforce had photos with Prak, Prak's mom, with strangers, with villagers he'd helped, even with a young Atiba himself. But there was nothing—not a single image—of his mother, Wilberforce's own daughter.

Atiba's chest tightened as the realization sank in. He had always known that his mother and grandfather had a strained relationship, but this… this was something else. It wasn't just a lack of closeness; it was an erasure. As if she had never existed in Wilberforce's life at all.

He stepped back, his mind racing. What could have driven such a deep rift between them? His mother had always been tight-lipped about her past, deflecting any questions about her father with sharp words or outright silence. Atiba had assumed it was just her usual bitterness, but now he wondered if there was more to it. Had Wilberforce done something to push her away? Or had she been the one to cut ties?

The questions swirled in his mind, but there were no answers to be found in the photographs. Just the silent, glaring absence of his mother's face.

Atiba sighed, running a hand through his hair. He felt a pang of guilt for even caring. His mother had never been particularly kind to him, and her obsession with Wilberforce's inheritance had left a sour taste in his mouth. But still… she was his mother. And seeing her so completely erased from this wall, from her own father's life, stirred something in him—a mix of sadness, anger, and curiosity.

He turned away from the wall, his eyes landing on the bangle that still hung from his wrist. The old, lacquered wood felt heavier now, as if it carried not just the weight of his grandfather's legacy, but the weight of all the unanswered questions that came with it.

Atiba walked over to the window, staring out at the village below. The sun was high in the sky now, casting a golden glow over the rooftops and the sea beyond. The sight should have been comforting, but Atiba felt anything but at ease.

Eventually he shook himself out of his thoughts and decided to clean up the place a little. The house was tidy, but it had the faint layer of dust that came with being uninhabited for a while. He figured it would be a good way to keep himself busy and maybe even feel a little more connected to the grandfather he barely remembered.

He started in the living room, dusting the shelves and wiping down the wooden surfaces with a damp cloth. The furniture was sturdy and well-made, but it had clearly seen better days. The armchair in the corner was worn but comfortable, its fabric soft from years of use. Atiba ran his hand over the back of the chair, imagining Wilberforce sitting there, reading one of the books that now lined the shelves.

Next, he moved to the kitchen, scrubbing the countertops and wiping down the stove. The cast-iron surface was smooth and well-seasoned, and the mason jars on the windowsill sparkled in the sunlight as he polished them. He opened the cabinets, finding them stocked with simple, practical dishes—plates, bowls, and cups, all well-used but cared for. It was a far cry from the sleek, modern kitchen he was used to back home, but there was something comforting about its simplicity.

As he worked, Atiba noticed something strange. At the threshold of each room, there was a thin line of what looked like salt. He crouched down, running his fingers through the fine white granules. Curious, he touched a bit to his tongue, confirming that it was indeed salt. He frowned, wondering why someone would have sprinkled salt in doorways. Was it some kind of local custom? A superstition? He didn't know, but it seemed out of place in the otherwise practical and no-nonsense atmosphere of the house.

Shrugging it off, Atiba grabbed a broom and swept the salt into a dustpan, dumping it into the trash. He continued his cleaning frenzy, mopping the floors and wiping down the walls until the house gleamed. By the time he was done, the place looked almost new, the wooden floors shining and the air fresh and clean.

Atiba stood in the middle of the living room, surveying his work. The house felt more like his now, less like a relic of a past he couldn't remember. The wooden floors gleamed, the air smelled fresh, and the faint layer of dust that had clung to everything was gone. He wiped his forehead with the back of his hand, feeling a small sense of accomplishment. But as he looked around, his eyes fell once again on the wall of photographs. The questions they raised still lingered in his mind, unanswered and unsettling.

He was about to turn away when something caught his eye—a faint glimmer on the floor near the doorway to the kitchen. He crouched down, running his fingers over the spot where he'd swept up the line of salt earlier. The granules were gone, but the floor felt… strange. Cold, almost unnaturally so, as if the warmth of the morning sun hadn't touched it. He frowned, pressing his palm flat against the wood. The chill seeped into his skin, sending a shiver up his arm.

Atiba straightened, shaking off the odd sensation. He told himself it was nothing, just his imagination running wild after the strange events of the morning. But as he turned to leave the room, he noticed something else—a faint, almost imperceptible sound, like the soft rustling of leaves or the whisper of fabric brushing against the floor. He froze, his heart skipping a beat.

"Hello?" he called out, his voice echoing in the empty house. There was no response, but the sound didn't stop. It seemed to be coming from the hallway, just out of sight. Atiba hesitated, his instincts warring with his curiosity. Part of him wanted to investigate, to prove to himself that there was nothing to be afraid of. But another part of him, the part that had seen a strange child vanish into the forest and felt the unnatural chill in the floor, urged him to stay put.

Before he could decide, the sound stopped. The house fell silent, the only noise the faint creak of the floorboards under his feet and the distant cry of a gull outside. Atiba let out a breath he didn't realize he'd been holding and shook his head. "Get it together, man," he muttered to himself. "It's just an old house. Old houses make noises."

He grabbed his phone (or rather, Prak's phone, since his own was still missing) and headed for the door. Stepping onto the veranda, he was greeted by the warm morning sun and the gentle rustle of the coconut palms. The village below was alive with activity—fishermen hauling their nets, children chasing each other through the streets, and the occasional crow of a rooster. It was a peaceful, ordinary scene, and Atiba felt some of the tension leave his shoulders.

As he stood there, taking in the view, his stomach growled loudly. He realized he hadn't eaten since the night before, and the thought of food was enough to distract him from the lingering unease. He decided to head down to the village and see if he could find something ready-made to eat.

But as he descended the steps, something made him pause. He glanced back at the house, his eyes drawn to the window of the living room. For a moment, he thought he saw something—a shadow moving behind the glass, quick and fleeting. He blinked, and it was gone.

Atiba shook his head, chiding himself for letting his imagination run wild. "Old houses," he muttered again, as if repeating it would make it true. He turned and made his way down the hill, the strange chill and the faint rustling already fading from his mind.

For now, at least.

# CHAPTER 4 - ESME

The dream always ended the same way. Esme stood before a massive, ancient tree, its gnarled roots burrowing deep into the earth, thick and unyielding, as though they had always been there. Its sprawling branches clawed at the sky, which hung too low, too heavy, pressing down with an oppressive weight. The air was thick with the scent of damp soil and decaying leaves, the hush of the forest broken only by the persistent hum of unseen insects.

She knew this place. Or at least, she felt like she did. It clung to the edges of her memory, just out of reach, teasing familiarity without offering certainty.

In the dream, she always moved forward, drawn toward the tree's base. The ground beneath her feet was soft, blanketed in moss that muffled her steps. And then there it was—the door. A simple wooden thing, weathered and rough, as though it had always been a part of the tree. It was slightly ajar, a faint, golden light pulsing from within, steady and rhythmic, like a heartbeat.

She would reach out. Her fingers would skim the surface, cool and splintered. She would push it open.

And then, Esme woke up.

Her cheek was stuck to the sticky surface of a table at Dougie's Bar, pressed into the damp ring left behind by a forgotten drink. The sharp, stale smell of alcohol clung to the air, mixing with the faint musk of sweat and wood varnish. A dull, insistent ache pulsed in her skull, radiating from her temples to the base of her neck. She groaned, peeling her face off the table and sitting up slowly, blinking against the harsh light filtering through the windows.

The bar was quiet. The low hum of a ceiling fan stirred the heavy air, and somewhere behind the counter, Dougie moved with sluggish purpose, glass clinking softly as he wiped them down.

Esme rubbed her face with both hands, trying to shake off the lingering haze of sleep. And then… Minnie.

The thought struck her like a punch to the gut.

She had thought threatening Duncan would scare him off, that it would be enough. But she had only fed his arrogance, made him reckless. The memory of Minnie's laughter flickered in her mind, her face bright, warm, alive. Then, just as quickly, the cold, impersonal tone of a news report. The words "strangled to death" still echoed in her ears.

Her chest tightened, a sharp pressure settling beneath her ribs. She swallowed hard, willing back the burn in her eyes. "Damn it," she muttered, her voice raw, unsteady.

Her fingers curled into fists against the table, nails biting into her palms. She had tried. She had tried. But it hadn't been enough. It never was.

A quiet shift in the air sent a ripple through her awareness. She wasn't alone.

Esme's muscles tensed instinctively as she lifted her gaze. Seated across from her was a woman who looked as though she had walked straight out of a corporate office.

Young. East Indian. Smooth, dark skin. Sharp features framed by a pair of delicate glasses resting on a thin chain. A crisp gray suit, neatly tailored, the kind worn by people who never had to break into a run. Her hands were folded neatly on the table, poised, patient.

Standing just behind her was a man, middle-aged, well-dressed, and far too pleased with himself. His cream-colored suit was expensive, tailored to a degree that made it clear he cared about appearances. His grin was wide and toothy, an expression that practically oozed impudence. Esme disliked him immediately.

Her instincts kicked in, shoving aside the remnants of her hangover. She sat up straighter, sharpening her focus, reaching for the power coiled deep in her chest—her Siren's Voice. She didn't hesitate.

The command formed on her tongue, smooth and insistent. A subtle shift in tone, in timbre, would be all it took to bend them to her will. She would tell them to leave. To forget they had ever seen her.

She spoke. Nothing happened.

The woman across from her tilted her head slightly, her lips curving into the faintest suggestion of a smile.

"A good effort," she said, her accent crisp, precise. Guyanese. "But your ability doesn't work when you've been drinking. That's why we chose now to approach you."

Esme's blood ran cold. She leaned back, her eyes narrowing. "Who is you? Yuh feel yuh could jus' siddown in front me so?" Her voice was low, dangerous.

"My name is Ms. Millicent," the woman replied, unruffled. "This is my associate, Mr. Heartmann. We're here on behalf of our employer, Mr. Brown."

Esme's jaw tightened. The fact that they knew about her ability, and its limitations, put her on edge. She glanced at Heartmann, who was still grinning, smug and unreadable. The kind of grin that made her fingers itch for violence.

"Mr. Brown?" she repeated, skepticism dripping from her tone. "Who de ass is dat, and wha' he want wit' me?"

Ms. Millicent leaned forward slightly. "Mr. Brown would like you to kill Papa Bois."

Silence.

Esme blinked, then let out a sharp, humorless laugh. "Aye, you mus' be mad, gyul. Who does just approach people an' ask dem to kill somebody? Carry yuhself from here, oui."

Ms. Millicent didn't flinch. "Mr. Brown is aware of your… situation. Specifically, your brother Levi."

The laughter died in Esme's throat. Her entire body went still.

"How the hell do you know about Levi?" she demanded, her voice quiet but laced with steel. The sudden switch from her usual dialect to proper English caused Ms. Millicent to smile slightly.

"Mr. Brown knows many things," The other woman replied smoothly. "He also knows that you and Levi were responsible for the Day of Darkness."

Esme's pulse skipped. She forced herself to remain still.

"That's bullshit," she said, but there was no conviction behind the words.

Millicent smiled.

"Levi can be helped. For a price."

Esme's fingers curled into fists beneath the table.

Levi's face flashed in her mind—his wide, unseeing eyes, the way he had looked at her the last time she had seen him. She had tried to fix what she had broken. Tried everything.

And now they were dangling hope in front of her.

"Even if I wanted to," she said slowly, choosing her words carefully. "I'm no match for the old man. I don't have a death wish."

Her mind spiraled back to the last time she had encountered Papa Bois.

Wilberforce DuBois was not a tall man, but he didn't need to be. His presence alone was enough to make the world feel smaller. His gaze burned with a righteous fury, his movements precise, calculated.

She had tried to run. She had always been fast, always been clever. But there was no escaping him. He moved like a force of nature, inevitable, unstoppable.

And yet—he hadn't killed her. He had let her go.

Even now, years later, the memory of his gaze still sent a chill through her. Ms. Millicent reached into her pocket and placed a phone on the table.

With a swipe, she pulled up a video and slid it toward Esme. Wilberforce's funeral.

Esme's breath caught in her throat.

"The old fool is dead," Ms. Millicent said. "Papa Bois is no more. This incarnation, at least."

She swiped again, revealing a new image: two young men sitting on the front steps of Wilberforce's house, drinking. "One of them is his successor," Millicent said. "If you accept our deal, it will be up to you to figure out which one... and kill them."

Esme stared at the photo and her stomach turned. Prak.

And next to him, the other... someone new. Lean like Prak but sharper at the edges, with brown skin and tight black curls that caught the light even through the phone's screen. His jaw was set, his dark eyes steady, holding something she couldn't quite read. Beside Prak's easy grin, he seemed the more guarded of the two.

Ms. Millicent slid a card across the table. "Think about it," she said. "From a practical standpoint, it's the only choice that makes sense."

Heartmann grinned at her once more before following his colleague out. Esme sat there, staring at the empty space where they had been. For the first time in a long time, she didn't know what to do.

# CHAPTER 5 - PRAK

Prak pulled the car to a stop at the side of the road, gravel crunching under the tires. He killed the engine and stepped out, stretching his arms above his head before rolling his shoulders to shake off the tension. Ahead, the forest stretched wide and deep, a living, breathing thing. The air buzzed with the chatter of birds and the rustling of unseen creatures in the undergrowth. Somewhere in the distance, a howler monkey bellowed its haunting call.

The morning sun filtered through the thick canopy, casting dappled shadows across the forest floor. The scent of damp earth, blooming flowers, and the musk of something wild filled Prak's lungs as he took a deep breath. This was home. Not the village, not the streets… this. The untamed, whispering depths of the bush.

Without hesitation, he sprinted forward, slipping into the trees with the fluidity of a predator on the hunt. His feet barely made a sound on the soft, mossy ground as he moved deeper into the forest. He reached the base of a towering samaan tree and, with a surge of power, leapt onto its thick trunk. His fingers dug into the rough bark, and he scaled it effortlessly, pulling himself onto a broad branch high above the ground.

From up here, the forest unfolded in a wild, chaotic sprawl of green, red, and gold. A hummingbird flitted past, a blur of iridescent blue. The leaves trembled with the movements of unseen creatures—agouti skittering in the underbrush, a coiled snake waiting in patient silence, a hawk circling far above.

Then, it began.

A ripple beneath his skin. A sudden, electric charge humming through his veins. His breath hitched as his nails sharpened into claws, his muscles thickened, his senses expanded until the world around him sharpened into perfect clarity.

He could feel the forest, the heart of it pulsing like a drumbeat in his chest. The scent of a wild hog drifted toward him, earthy and pungent, somewhere far off. A lizard scurried up a tree, its tiny claws scratching against the bark. Even the faint hum of insects took on a layered rhythm.

This was not a grotesque transformation. He did not become monstrous. He became primal. Instinct took the lead, though it no longer consumed him like it once had.

That control had been hard-won.

Prak remembered the early days, the ones filled with fear and confusion. Waking up deep in the bush, his body covered in the blood of an unfortunate animal, with no memory of what had happened. The night when he had nearly killed a villager, his mind aware but his body ruled by hunger. If it hadn't been for Levi and Darren—his brothers in all but blood—there would have been no coming back from that.

He shook off the memory. Not today.

Focusing on the task at hand, he leaped from the branch, landing silently on another, and continued moving through the canopy.

He thought of Wilberforce. Of the countless walks they had taken through this very forest. The old man had been a guide, a guardian, a force of wisdom and strength in his life. His death had left a void that Prak wasn't sure he could fill.

But he had to try.

For the village. For his family. For himself.

Eventually, he reached a clearing. At its center stood a small, ramshackle hut, its wooden walls weathered and warped with age, its roof sagging under the weight of time. Just outside, a group of children played, their laughter ringing through the trees.

But these were no ordinary children. They wore large, floppy straw hats that hid their faces. Their feet, backward, with heels where toes should have been, gave them away.

Douen. Mischievous spirits, known for leading children astray, luring them deep into the forest with playful giggles and ghostly whispers.

Prak's eyes narrowed.

Wilberforce had brokered an old deal, a pact that kept them in check. But now, with the old man gone, the balance was shifting. And the Douen were testing the limits.

He dropped from the trees without warning, landing among them in a crouch. The Douen scattered instantly, their laughter warping into startled cries as they vanished into the underbrush. Prak barely spared them a glance. His focus was on the hut. His body shrank back to its human form, claws retracting, muscles settling. Straightening, he stepped forward and knocked on the door with a deliberate, firm rhythm.

A beat of silence.

Then, a voice... low, gravelly, and unimpressed. "Enter."

Prak pushed the door open and stepped inside.

The first thing that hit him was the smell. A thick, cloying mix of earth, rot, and something metallic... blood. It coated the air, worming its way into his lungs. The dim interior flickered with the weak glow of a single oil lamp, casting long, distorted shadows against the walls.

Shelves lined with old jars stretched from floor to ceiling, each container filled with murky, unidentifiable liquids. Some held twisted roots suspended in amber fluid; others housed things that should not have been preserved, fetal creatures with too many limbs, shriveled black hearts, the cloudy, disembodied gaze of something once alive staring out from the glass.

Bundles of dried herbs and bones hung from the rafters, swaying slightly, though there was no breeze. A massive iron pot sat in the corner atop a smoldering fire, its contents bubbling thick and slow, releasing a pungent steam that stung Prak's eyes.

And at the center of it all, hunched over a battered wooden table, was her.

The old woman tore into a hunk of raw, bloodied meat, her dark, pockmarked skin glistening with sweat. The muscles in her thin, wiry arms flexed as she worked her teeth through sinew and flesh, each bite wet and deliberate. She didn't stop when Prak entered. Didn't even acknowledge him at first.

He took a slow step inside, letting the door creak shut behind him. The floor groaned under his weight.

Finally, she lifted her gaze.

Her eyes were small, bead-like, gleaming with an eerie sharpness in the dim light. She wiped her mouth lazily with the back of her hand, smearing blood across her chin, then leaned back in her chair, exhaling through her nose like a predator that had just finished feeding.

A slow, knowing smile curled across her lips.

"Well, well. Look who decide to grace meh humble abode." Her voice was thick with amusement, laced with something condescending. Testing.

Prak didn't sit. He didn't move any closer. He could feel the wrongness of this place pressing in around him, thick and suffocating. It wasn't just the smell, or the dim light, or the grotesque relics that lined the shelves. It was alive.

Something in the walls. The floorboards. The air itself. Watching. Waiting.

Prak ignored it. Ignored the way the shadows in the corners of the room felt too deep, too still. Instead, he kept his gaze locked onto the old woman, his tone firm.

"One ah yuh Douen reach de main road."

The words cut through the silence like the crack of a branch in an empty forest.

The woman's expression didn't change, but there was a shift. A slow, subtle tension that coiled in the space between them.

"Doh let dat happen again."

The old woman's smile widened. Not pleasant. Teeth too sharp, too white against her dark gums. "Now dat Papa Bois dead," she said, voice smooth as oil, "wha' mek yuh tink ah owe yuh any respect? Yuh eh no big man yet, boy."

Prak's jaw tightened.

"Yuh made an oath to meh grandfather," he said evenly. "Ah here to remind yuh ah dat."

The woman sucked her teeth, the sharp sound cutting through the heavy air. She sat forward slightly, placing both hands on the table—long, knotted fingers, nails yellowed and curling slightly at the edges, stained dark from years of handling things best left untouched.

"Wilberforce dead," she repeated, the weight behind her words heavier this time. "Watch yuh tone before ah show yuh what disrespect gets yuh."

The room felt smaller.

The fire in the iron pot roared to life without warning, a sudden flare of heat licking at the ceiling. The air thickened, vibrating with unseen energy.

And then, her mouth split apart.

Not a human mouth. Not even close.

Her jaw unhinged, widening far beyond natural limits, stretching grotesquely down her neck, revealing an abyss of burning light. Deep within, something flickered, shifting and writhing like a fire trapped beneath her skin.

The scent of scorched herbs filled the hut. Heat pressed against Prak's skin, but he didn't move. Didn't flinch.

Instead, he let his own power rise.

A slow breath. A ripple beneath his skin. His muscles tightened, his claws extended, his eyes burned with an unnatural glow. He let the transformation creep just enough to remind her who she was dealing with.

The fire in her mouth pulsed.

A test. A challenge. Who would break first? Prak held her gaze, unyielding.

"Dis de third an' las' time ah sayin' it," he said, voice low, steady, certain.

"Keep yuh Douen in check."

The old woman's fiery maw pulsed again, once… twice… then slowly, dimmed. Her mouth snapped shut with an audible click.

And then, she laughed. Not a cackle. Not mocking. Something else. Something heavier.

"Eh-eh," she murmured, shaking her head, the tension in the room loosening just a fraction. "Yuh grandfather woulda be proud. Yuh have steel in yuh spine, boy."

She leaned back again, the shadows around her settling. The fire in the pot returned to its slow, lazy bubbling.

She waved a dismissive hand. "Ah was jus' jokin', eh. Yuh doh hadda get so serious. De Douen go behave deyself."

Prak didn't respond. He didn't trust the sudden shift.

The woman studied him a moment longer, then smirked. "Yuh feel it, right?" she murmured. "Wha' yuh friend do, it tear de veil. Spirits, jumbies, all kinda ting creeping through. And Wilberforce was de only one keepin' it all in check."

Prak's fists clenched at his sides.

She watched him carefully, then exhaled through her nose, the amusement in her gaze darkening into something sharper.

"Anyone who try to take advantage ah Boisdepin hadda go through me first," Prak said.

The old woman tilted her head, considering him. And then, for the first time, there was something almost approving in her expression.

"Yuh grandfather teach yuh good," she admitted. "But yuh eh have he wisdom. Not yet."

She reached into the folds of her ragged dress and pulled out something small, tossing it onto the table with a soft clack.

Prak glanced down. A cell phone. Atiba's.

"Yuh cousin lose dis," she said casually. "Tell him to be more careful next time. De forest doh play nice wit' strangers."

Prak hesitated, then picked up the phone, slipping it into his pocket. As he turned to leave, the old woman chuckled.

"De forest watching, boy. And so am I."

Prak didn't look back as he stepped out of the hut and into the clearing. The heavy air of the cramped space clung to him, thick with the scent of burning herbs and something far older, something ancient and watching. The moment he crossed the threshold, the temperature seemed to shift, the weight of unseen eyes pressing down on his shoulders.

The Douen were gone. Not a single trace of them remained. The silence was unsettling. No laughter, no whispering footsteps retreating into the brush. Just absence.

Prak exhaled slowly, releasing the tension coiled tight in his chest. The cool forest air filled his lungs, sharp and grounding, washing away the lingering scent of blood and charred magic. He clenched his fists, forcing himself to focus. The Douen would be kept in check. For now. But there was no victory in this.

As he made his way back to the trees, the old woman's words echoed in his mind, curling like vines around his thoughts.

"The veil is torn. The balance is shifting."

Wilberforce had been the anchor—the force that held the creeping chaos of the unseen world at bay. With him gone, the rules were unraveling. Old agreements were breaking. Spirits that had once slumbered were waking.

Prak felt it in his bones, in the way the forest watched him now, the way it whispered warnings he couldn't yet understand.

And it was up to him to hold it together. But not forever.

Prak leaped into the canopy, catching onto a thick branch, his body moving on instinct. He swung to the next, landing with the ease of someone who had spent his life in the trees. His car was still miles away, but he knew every inch of this forest, every pathway hidden beneath the tangle of roots and vines. His body moved with purpose, but his mind churned.

Atiba didn't know. He had no idea that the weight of Boisdepin, the duty, the protection, the burden was his to bear.

Prak had been trying to figure out how to tell him, how to prepare him. Because once he did, once Atiba knew, his life as he understood it would be over.

He had just met his cousin, but he already liked him. And that made it worse.

Wilberforce had prepared him for this moment. Before he died, the old man had pulled him aside, his voice steady, unshaken.

"He is the one, Prak. It won't be you. But I am proud of you, boy. More than you know. Guide him. Watch over him. Help him carry what is coming. Until he is ready you bridge the gap."

Prak had accepted those words in the moment, but now they weighed on him like iron. Atiba had no clue what was coming for him. No idea that everything he knew was about to be stripped away, replaced by a reality he hadn't chosen.

And Prak would be the one to deliver that truth.

The old woman's warning rang in his ears once again.

"The balance is shifting. The veil is torn. And Boisdepin is ripe for the picking."

The forest stretched out before him, alive and breathing beneath the morning sun. It pulsed with something ancient, something waiting.

Prak moved through the trees with practiced ease, his heart pounding, not from exertion, but from the weight of what lay ahead.

Atiba wasn't ready.

So until he was, Prak would stand in the space between. He would hold the line, fight the fights, keep the world from collapsing into something his cousin wouldn't be able to save.

He would make sure that when Atiba stepped into his birthright, he would have something left to protect.

# CHAPTER 6 - ATIBA

As Atiba walked, the warm Caribbean breeze brushed against his face. Boisdepin in all of its simple splendor stretched out before him, a patchwork of colorful houses, winding dirt roads, and lush greenery. He took a deep breath, savoring the scent of saltwater and blooming flowers, and began his descent down the hill. The pace was slow, deliberate, allowing him to take in the rural charm of the place. It was so different from Queens, where the streets were crowded, the air thick with the hum of traffic and the chatter of people always in a hurry. Here, life seemed to move at its own rhythm, unhurried and unburdened.

As he walked, Atiba couldn't help but feel a quiet sense of pride. The house, his house, was finally clean, the air inside fresh, the wooden floors gleaming under the light. That was still strange to think about. His house. Wilberforce had left it to him. Not his mother. Not anyone else. And the longer he stayed in Trinidad, in Boisdepin, the more that truth settled into him like roots digging into the earth.

It wasn't just a house. It was history. A connection to something bigger than himself, to a lineage he was only beginning to grasp. He had spent his whole life feeling like an outsider to this place, like he didn't quite belong here. But now? Now, he wanted to know more. He needed to.

But that pride was quickly swallowed by a wave of melancholy.

His mother had already made her intentions clear. She wanted the house sold. The land, the structure, everything… gone to the highest bidder.

It was just property to her. A number on a page. An asset to be cashed out and forgotten.

But to Atiba, it was more.

It was the scent of old wood and open windows. It was the wall of photographs that told the story of generations before him. It was Wilberforce, his presence woven into every nail, every beam, every tile. The thought of some stranger coming in, gutting it, tearing it down, or worse… letting it fall into ruin, left a hollow ache in his chest.

Still, he knew how this would end. His mother wasn't changing her mind. He had no way to fight her on it. And even if he did, assuming she still took whatever money he got aside from the house, he had no money to pay for upkeep, no resources to cover repairs. Keeping the house meant maintaining it, and maintaining it meant stability. Something he didn't have.

The weight of that truth pressed down on him as he wandered further into the village. And for the first time, he began to understand why Wilberforce hadn't kept a single photograph of his mother on that wall. Why, in a house filled with family, she was the one face missing.

Maybe, just maybe, he was beginning to see why his grandfather had chosen to erase her.

The sound of chatter and the faint smell of fried food drew his attention to a small corner shop. It was little more than a shack, its wooden walls weathered but sturdy, with a corrugated tin roof that gleamed in the sunlight. A makeshift sign hung above the entrance, advertising "Bake and Saltfish" in bold, hand-painted letters. Atiba's stomach growled at the sight.

It was the only thing on the menu he recognized, thanks to his mother making it frequently when he was growing up. He stepped inside.

The shop was dimly lit, the air thick with the scent of spices and frying oil. Behind the counter sat an old man, his face obscured behind an open newspaper. He didn't look up as Atiba approached, his attention seemingly absorbed by whatever he was reading.

"Uh, hello," Atiba said, clearing his throat. "Can I get a bake and saltfish?"

The old man grunted, not lowering the newspaper. "Barbra," he called out, his voice gruff and gravelly.

A moment later, a woman emerged from the back room. She wasn't tall, but she carried herself with such unshakable ease that the space seemed to open around her. Sunlight spilled through the front window, glancing off her skin—deep and rich as polished mahogany—and caught in the loose curls that slipped free from the bright bandana tied around her head. Her frame was full and soft, her movements measured and sure, the kind that made her presence feel steady, rooted. Her eyes were wide, curious, and kind—though there was a glint in them, a spark that hinted she could match wit for wit if she chose.

She draped an apron over her clothes as she greeted Atiba warmly, her Trinidadian accent melodic and inviting, each word flowing with the easy rhythm of familiarity. "Good mornin'! One bake and saltfish comin' right up," she said, already moving to prepare the dish. "Ah see yuh new around here. Yuh here for de funeral?"

Atiba nodded, leaning against the counter. "Yeah. Wilberforce was my grandfather."

Barbra paused, her expression softening. "Ah sorry for yuh loss. Yuh grandfather was a good man. Gruff, yes, but always nice. When ah was small, he used to give me sweets and let me rub he beard. It was so prickly!" She laughed, the sound light and infectious. "Ah used to call him 'Prickly Grandpa,' but he didn't mind. He just laugh and say, 'Dat's right, chile. Prickly like de forest.'"

Atiba listened, a faint smile tugging at his lips. It was strange, hearing stories about his grandfather from someone else's perspective. Prak had already painted a picture of Wilberforce as a stern but fair man, but Barbra's words added a new layer: one of a man who, despite his gruff exterior, had a soft spot for children.

As Barbra chattered away, Atiba found himself enamored by the way she spoke. Her Trinidadian accent was like a song, each word flowing into the next with a rhythm and cadence that was utterly captivating. It was so different from the way his mother spoke, her accent hardened by years of living in New York. Barbra's voice was warm, inviting, and it made him feel at ease in a way he hadn't felt since arriving in Trinidad, or at least since that first beer with Prak.

When she finally handed him the bake and saltfish, he thanked her and took a bite. The flavors exploded in his mouth… the flaky bake, the savory saltfish, the hint of spice. It was perfect. He ate quickly, savoring every bite, while Barbra continued to talk, her energy seemingly boundless.

"Ah name Barbra, by de way," she said, leaning on the counter. "After Barbra Streisand. Meh mudda love 'Hello Dolly', but ah eh never see it. Ah always mean to, though."

Atiba chuckled, wiping his mouth with a napkin. "Well, if you ever get around to it, let me know what you think."

Barbra then gestured to the old man. "Dis is meh fadda, Sheldon. But everybody does call he Donny. Funny, right? Yuh would tink dey go call he Shelly, but he eh like dat. So he force everybody to call he Donny."

"My name's Atiba," the young man chuckled, glancing at Donny. "Nice to meet you both, Donny, Barbra."

The old man behind the newspaper finally lowered it, revealing a weathered face with sharp, observant eyes. "Allyuh used to play together when yuh was small," he said, his voice cutting through the conversation like a knife.

Atiba blinked, caught off guard. "What?"

The old man didn't elaborate. Instead, he stood and disappeared into the back room, leaving Atiba and Barbra staring after him in confusion. A few moments later, he returned, holding an old photograph. He handed it to Atiba without a word.

The photo was faded, its edges worn, but the image was clear enough. It showed two children, no more than three years old, standing side by side in the front yard of Wilberforce's house. One was a little girl with a wide, gap-toothed smile. The other was a little boy, his face serious but his eyes bright with curiosity. Atiba recognized the boy immediately. It was him. And the girl… he glanced up at Barbra, who was peering over his shoulder.

"Dat's me!" she exclaimed, pointing at the little girl in the photo. "Look how small ah was! And da'is you, eh!"

Atiba stared at the photo with a neutral expression. He had no memory of this moment, no memory of Barbra or playing in his grandfather's yard. But there it was, one more photograph that proved that he had been here, that he had been a part of this place once. The realization left him feeling both unsettled and strangely comforted.

"Guess we go way back," Barbra said, her smile widening. "Small world, eh?"

Atiba nodded, handing the photo back to the old man. "Yeah. Small world."

Barbra leaned back against the counter, arms folded, eyes glinting with curiosity. "So if yuh Wilberforce grandson, dat mean yuh Prak cousin, eh? Well, I shoulda known. Ah could see de resemblance." She tilted her head slightly, looking him over like she was studying some long-lost connection.

Then, with a dramatic sigh, she shook her head, a slow smile creeping onto her lips. "Before, he was a real quiet chile. Hardly used to talk, but somehow always endin' up in some kinda trouble. If someting break, was Prak. If somebody get vex, was Prak. Dat boy was like a magnet for bacchanal." She chuckled to herself, shaking her head again. "But now? Eh-eh! He real step up." There was admiration in her tone, genuine pride in the way she spoke. "Always de first one to show up when somebody need help. Always doin' someting for de village. He even handle all de arrangements for yuh grandfaddah funeral, make sure everything went smooth. He reliable now, yuh know?" She nodded, as if reassuring herself. "Man like dat rare."

Atiba raised an eyebrow, amused by her enthusiasm. "Yeah, I've noticed. Prak's a good guy. I'm lucky to have him as a cousin."

Barbra's smile widened. "Yuh lucky, yes. He's one ah de good ones." Then, with a teasing spark in her eye, she leaned in just slightly, lowering her voice as if sharing a secret. "Tell me someting, though… yuh get de same family genes, or what? 'Cause Prak lookin' like a whole meal these days."

Atiba let out a short laugh, shaking his head. "I guess you'll have to judge that for yourself."

Barbra gasped playfully, pressing a hand to her chest. "Oh, so yuh leavin' it up to me to decide? Alright, alright." She grinned, nudging him with her elbow before straightening up. "Ah go be watchin' and seein' den." Her laughter was light, easy, like she truly enjoyed the conversation.

Atiba offered a small nod in response and planted a crisp $20 note on the counter. "I should get going. Thanks for the food."

Barbra sucked her teeth and shook her head, crossing her arms. "No family of Wilberforce go ever have to pay to eat here. Keep it."

Atiba hesitated, his fingers lingering over the bill. "Nah, I insist—"

Before he could finish, Donny lowered his newspaper again, fixing him with a pointed, unwavering stare. The kind that needed no words. The kind that made it clear arguing was not an option.

Atiba swallowed, nodding quickly as he sheepishly scooped the money back up. "T-thanks!"

Barbra smirked, clearly amused. "Doh mention it, city boy."

Donny gave a satisfied grunt and returned to his reading, leaving Atiba to make his exit with the quiet understanding that in this village, respect and gratitude held far more weight than money ever could.

Atiba stepped out of the shop, the midday sun hitting his skin as he started walking. He didn't have a destination in mind. He just wanted to see the village, not just in passing, not just as a visitor, but as someone who was trying to belong.

He followed winding side streets, taking the smaller trails that splintered off from the main road, paths that led between houses, behind gardens, down to places he had no name for. Some led to quiet dead ends where old, abandoned structures sat nestled in overgrown bush. Others curved around hills, giving him glimpses of Boisdepin from different angles, different perspectives.

Everywhere he went, he waved at the people he passed. Old women sitting in their porches watching the road. Children darting between houses, playing barefoot in the dirt. Men fixing fences, carrying bags of provisions, tending to small backyard crops. Some waved back, some only nodded in acknowledgment.

The animals didn't pay him any mind. Chickens pecked lazily at the roadside, stray dogs lounged in patches of shade, and goats stood in clusters on the hillsides, chewing absentmindedly. He stayed out of their way, letting the rhythm of village life flow around him.

Eventually, he made his way to the beach.

The scent of salt filled the air, stronger than it had been up on the hill. The sand was warm under his feet, the grains shifting softly as he stepped onto the shore. The water stretched endlessly before him, the waves rolling in with a steady, calming rhythm.

He walked closer, stepping into the surf until the water lapped around his knees. The coolness was refreshing, grounding.

He let himself take it all in: the way the sun glinted off the waves, the way the horizon seemed impossibly far away. This was something he had never seen growing up in Queens. The ocean had always been a distant thing, something confined to trips or summer outings. Here, it was different. It belonged.

For a moment, he let himself wonder if he could belong too. But that moment passed, and after a while, he turned back toward the village, making his way inland.

The cemetery at the edge of Boisdepin was old, older than the village itself, he'd heard some of the villagers say when they buried his grandfather. It sat behind a rusted iron gate, its bars twisted and worn with age, barely clinging to their original shape. Beyond the entrance, uneven rows of weathered headstones and above-ground tombs stretched across the field, some standing proudly, others leaning slightly, their edges softened by time.

The scent of damp earth and drying grass lingered in the air, carried by the occasional breeze that stirred the hanging branches of the massive trees.

Some plots were well-tended, with fresh flowers placed at their bases, candles long since burned out resting beside them. Others were forgotten, overtaken by creeping vines and the weight of neglect.

Atiba hesitated as he came toward the entrance, his fingers tightening at his sides. He hadn't come here since the funeral. Hadn't wanted to. But now, standing at the threshold, the weight of obligation settled over him. He was already here, he might as well pay his respects.

Taking a slow breath, he stepped through the gate. The dirt path crunched beneath his sneakers as he moved carefully between the rows, his eyes scanning the names carved into the stones.

Then he saw it. Wilberforce's grave.

It was a newer plot, the headstone freshly carved, the soil still settling from the burial a few days prior.

But Atiba wasn't alone.

A woman stood before the grave, her posture relaxed yet her expression unreadable. She was short and curvy, with dark chocolate skin and wild black hair that spilled out from beneath a bright yellow bandana. A black t-shirt and fitted jeans hugged her figure, simple and unassuming. She didn't cry, didn't speak. She simply stood there, her gaze fixed on the stone.

Atiba slowed his steps, unsure if he should interrupt. Instead, he waited, watching her.

She wasn't family. He was sure of that. He had met most of the relatives at the funeral, and she hadn't been among them. But there was something about her, something intense, something unreadable, that made him pause.

Who was she?

As if sensing his presence, the woman turned toward him. Her dark eyes flicked over him, taking him in. She seemed momentarily surprised to see him there, but the emotion passed quickly, replaced by something calmer, more measured.

"Yuh come to pay yuh respects too?" she asked, her voice smooth, lilting with the melody of Trinidad.

Atiba hesitated before nodding. "Yeah."

She studied him for a moment, then exhaled, offering a quiet, "My condolences."

"Thanks," he said.

For a few moments, neither of them spoke. The only sounds were the rustling leaves, and the distant chirping of birds.

Finally, Atiba broke the silence. "How did you know him?"

The woman's gaze flickered, as if debating how much to say. Then, with a small, almost wry smile, she answered. "We was enemies."

Atiba blinked, caught off guard. "Enemies?"

She gave a small nod, her voice calm but firm. "We was on different sides of… a family dispute. My family, not his… But even when ah give him reason not to trust meh, he always treat meh fair." She turned back toward the grave, her expression softening just slightly. "Ah respect him. An' ah sorry ah cyah benefit from he wisdom no more."

Atiba took in her words, curiosity prickling at the back of his mind. She spoke about Wilberforce with an air of familiarity, but also distance. Not like someone who had been close to him, but someone who had known him well enough, someone who had stood across from him in ways others hadn't.

For reasons he couldn't explain, he didn't doubt her sincerity. "I'm Atiba," he said finally, extending a hand.

The woman turned toward him again, looking at his outstretched palm for a second before shaking it. Her grip was firm, her touch warm.

"Esme Walcott."

As their hands parted, her eyes flickered down to his wrist, to the wooden bangle he wore and her gaze lingered on it with quiet recognition.

"Ah see Wilberforce wear dat before," she said. "He leave it to yuh?" Atiba glanced at the bangle before nodding. "Yeah."

A long silence stretched between them.

Then, Esme asked, "Yuh see or hear anything strange since yuh start wearin' it?"

Atiba tensed.

His mind immediately flickered back to the funeral. To the elk that had appeared before him in the church. The elk that no one else had seen.

"I…" He hesitated.

Esme's voice softened. "Yuh could tell meh. Ah eh go tink yuh mad."

There was something reassuring about her tone. Something that made him want to trust her. So, he told her.

She listened without interrupting, her expression unreadable. Then, after a long pause, she spoke.

"Stop breathing."

Atiba frowned. "What?"

Her voice was calm, almost casual. "Jus' stop breathing."

The request was bizarre. It wasn't a command, there was no urgency, no explanation. Just the suggestion, gentle and simple.

Atiba started to ask why, but the awkwardness of the situation kept him quiet. The moment stretched.

Nothing happened.

Esme chuckled softly. "Yeah. Ah know it wouldn't work. But was worth a try."

Atiba shook his head, thoroughly confused. "What exactly were you trying?"

She met his gaze, and her next words sent a chill down his spine. "Confirmin' what ah already know. You is Wilberforce successor. You's de new Papa Bois."

Atiba stared at her, the words sounding foreign, meaningless. His brows knitted together as he let out a short laugh—not of amusement, but exasperation.

"I'm the what?"

Esme tilted her head slightly, her dark eyes searching his face as though she were trying to gauge if he was being serious.

"Papa Bois," she repeated, slower this time, like it should mean something to him.

But it didn't. Atiba shook his head. "I don't know what that is." Esme exhaled through her nose, her lips pressing into a thin line.

"Wilberforce ain't tell yuh nothin'?"

Atiba's frustration flared. He spread his hands, his voice sharper now. "I never met the man! At least not when I was old enough to remember him."

Esme let out a soft, dry laugh. "Well, dat explain plenty."

Atiba's chest tightened. The way she said it, like she knew something he didn't, something important… only made his frustration grow.

"Explain what?"

She looked at him again, and this time, there was something close to pity in her expression. Not quite sympathy, not quite regret.

She shook her head. "Ah sorry."

Atiba felt his stomach turn. "For what?"

Before she could answer, the ground beneath him shifted. It was subtle at first—a whisper of movement, like the earth had taken a breath.

He stood in the shade of a massive headstone, the towering tree beside it stretching its branches wide, casting speckled darkness across the graveyard. The shadow pooled thickly around his feet, stretching across Wilberforce's plot, deep and unmoving, as if the very earth had swallowed the light whole. It was darker than it should have been.

Too still. Too heavy.

Then, in a horrifying instant, the shadow began to move. It rippled first, a slow, unnatural tremor. Then it swirled, twisting like black ink bleeding into water. And before Atiba could react, it pulled him down.

His breath caught as his legs were quickly swallowed up by thick, dark-purple sludge, bubbling and oozing like quicksand.

Atiba panicked.

His hands clawed at the ground, but there was nothing solid to grasp. He was sinking, fast.

"Esme!" His voice cracked with terror. He thrust out a hand toward her. "Help me!"

She didn't move.

She only watched, her expression unreadable.

"Ah go make sure dey find yuh body at least," she said quietly. "So yuh could get a proper burial."

Her words were tinged with sadness. But only barely. And then, the darkness swallowed him whole.

# CHAPTER 7 - PRAK

The road back to Boisdepin blurred past Prak, but he barely noticed. His grip on the steering wheel was vice-like, his knuckles white as his fingers dug into the leather. His jaw was clenched so tightly it ached, his teeth grinding together as his thoughts churned like a storm. The old woman's warning echoed in his mind, her voice eerily calm, too certain, too resigned, like she had already accepted the fate she had seen.

And that was what unsettled him the most. Wilberforce had been the anchor, the one who kept the worst of the Day of Darkness contained. He had held the veil in place, keeping the chaos at bay. But the old man was dead, and Prak could feel the weight of something cracking, splitting, unraveling. The balance was shifting, and he wasn't sure he was strong enough to hold it together.

Then the scent hit him. Familiar.

Unwelcome.

Hated.

His lips curled back in a silent snarl, and an ugly hiss escaped his throat. The sound was primal, raw, filled with an emotion Prak barely recognized in himself. He had been angry before. He had been furious before. But this?

This was hatred. His foot slammed down on the accelerator, and the car lurched forward, tearing through the winding roads of the village like a beast on the hunt. He didn't even think. He just drove. Dirt and gravel kicked up violently as the vehicle roared toward the scent's origin. His instincts screamed. His muscles tensed. He already knew where he was going.

The cemetery. Prak's gut twisted. No.

The car skidded violently to a stop just outside the cemetery, its tires spitting rocks and dust into the air. Prak didn't bother turning off the engine.

Didn't bother closing the door. He was already running. His legs pounded against the earth, his heart thundering in his chest.

Esme's scent was thick, clinging to the air like rot. But something else flickered beneath it. Something fainter, more recent.

Atiba.

His stomach plummeted.

His cousin had been here. Had been. But when Prak's eyes swept the graveyard, he wasn't here anymore.

His feet carried him forward before he even realized it, straight to the freshest grave in the cemetery.

Wilberforce's grave.

And standing in front of it, alone, was her. Esme.

Prak skidded to a stop, his chest heaving, his body coiled with tension.

Whatever she'd done to Atiba, she hadn't moved. Hadn't fled. She just stood there, her hands at her sides, her expression unreadable. Why?

Why the hell was she here?

Before he could voice the question, she answered it herself as if she had been waiting for him to ask.

"Was foolish," she murmured, her voice soft but steady. "Ah know it was. But..." she exhaled, and for the first time since he had arrived, she looked almost... small. "Ah just wanted to see yuh, Prak. After all dis time."

Prak stilled.

She had wanted to see him? His fury surged.

"Why?" he growled, his voice a dangerous rumble. "So yuh could look meh in de eye after what yuh just do?"

She let out a small, humorless chuckle.

"Yuh look real different now," she said instead, "but ah could still tell it's you. Strong. Steady. Yuh remind meh of Darren, yuh know?"

Something snapped.

Prak's entire body went rigid, his breath sharp, his claws flexing at his sides.

"Keep Darren name out yuh mouth," he snarled, each word dripping with venom.

Esme didn't flinch. She only nodded, accepting his anger. "Fair."

The young man's chest rose and fell in deep, heavy breaths, his fingers twitching as his control frayed. A long silence stretched between them.

Then, her voice came soft, steady. "Yuh cousin, Atiba was it? Ah trade he life fuh Levi's."

The shift in Prak was instant. His entire body locked up, his muscles coiled, every fiber of him screaming in violent protest. "What?" His voice was barely more than a whisper, but the rage beneath it trembled like an earthquake.

She sighed. "Ah make a deal."

And then she told him. The agents. The man called Mr. Brown. The knowledge they already had—about her past, her abilities, Atiba, Prak, Levi. As she spoke, Prak's claws curled tighter, his breathing grew heavier, his vision darkened.

"You's a fool," he spat, his voice like a blade. "Yuh really believe dem? Yuh really tink some random man go just fix what you did to Levi?"

Esme didn't answer.

"Bring Atiba back. Now."

She ignored him.

"Levi was extraordinarily prodigious with the use of his shadow ability," she said, switching to proper English. "But I've learned a thing or two myself after inheriting it."

And then Prak noticed it.

The ground trembled. A deep, subtle hum slithered through the air, something just on the edge of perception.

His eyes snapped downward.

Thin, inky tendrils stretched from Esme's shadow, weaving through his own and sprawling outward, a web spread across the entire cemetery.

His pulse spiked. "No," he breathed.

Then the graves burst open.

The earth erupted, sending dirt and mud flying. And from the open graves, they crawled out.

Twenty bodies.

Each one wrapped in a solid, shifting mass of darkness—a living, writhing abyss stitched to their decaying flesh and bones. Within the shadows, patterns flickered, nebulae twisting, constellations winking in and out of existence. The night sky had been pulled from the heavens and twisted into something unholy.

Prak staggered back, his breath shaky, his heart hammering. He whipped his gaze to Wilberforce's grave. It was untouched. Esme hadn't desecrated him. That was the only mercy in this nightmare.

"Let meh walk away, Prak," she said quietly. "Ah cousin yuh barely know eh worth more dan yuh own best friend. Yuh own sworn bredren?"

Something wavered inside him. The thought of Levi being at his side in the mess he'd inherited sent a pang of longing through his very soul. But only for a moment. Then his resolve hardened.

"You and Levi cause de Day of Darkness. Wilberforce keep de damage from spreadin'. He hold de veil in place. But now he gone."

His claws flexed.

"If yuh take Atiba out de picture, dis eh just Trinidad problem. Dis de world problem."

Esme sighed.

"If dat's true… den me and Levi go fix it. Together." She took a slow step backward. "Ah hoped yuh woulda help too."

Then, her voice dropped. "Subdue him. But doh kill him."

The first of the shadow-wrapped corpses lunged. Its movements were jerky, unnatural—but disturbingly fast. Prak sidestepped, his claws slashing deep through the shifting darkness that clung to its form. The shadow hissed and recoiled, writhing like a wounded beast. Beneath it, the rotting corpse crumpled, lifeless once more.

Two more surged from opposite sides, their eyes hollow, their bodies wrapped in living, undulating blackness. Prak dropped low, sweeping his leg in a wide arc. The first stumbled, its legs knocked out from under it. Before it could react, Prak sprang up, claws raking down in a vicious, downward strike.

His claws ripped through its chest, the shadow armor writhing as if in pain. With a deep snarl, he yanked his claws free. The corpse collapsed in a heap, unmoving.

A third corpse swung wildly, its fist wrapped in pure darkness. Prak ducked just in time, the force of the strike brushing his shoulder like a gust of wind. He countered with a brutal uppercut, his claws tearing through its jaw with a sickening crunch. The force of the blow sent it sprawling, but even as it fell, four more were already closing in.

Prak crouched low, scanning their movements. Each was waiting for the perfect moment to strike. They were learning. Adapting.

The first lunged, and Prak met it head-on, his claws tearing through its shadowy form. The second attacked from behind—Prak's ears twitched at the shift in air. He whipped around, his tail lashing out like a whip, knocking it off balance. The third charged at his moment of distraction.

Prak turned—too slow. It tackled him hard, driving him backward into a headstone with enough force to crack the stone in half. Pain exploded through his spine, but he gritted his teeth.

Before the corpse could pin him, he thrust both clawed hands into its chest and ripped it apart. The shadow armor screamed—and the corpse crumbled into nothing.

The next was smaller than the rest—a woman. She had once been someone's mother, someone's sister. Prak recognized her face beneath the shadows. A woman who used to bring him sugar cakes when he was a boy. His stomach twisted.

She lunged…and Prak hesitated. That half-second of hesitation cost him.

Another corpse rammed into his side, knocking the wind out of him. His feet skidded against the mud, and before he could react, another clawed hand wrapped around his throat. Pain shot through his windpipe as the shadow tendrils tightened like a noose.

Prak choked, his lungs screaming for air. His vision blurred at the edges. He began to panic.

No! Not like this!

With one last burst of strength, Prak drove his knee into the creature's stomach, twisting viciously until he broke free.

He staggered, gasping for breath. They weren't giving him time to recover. He had to end this now.

He let out a slow, rumbling growl, a sound that vibrated through his entire chest. Then, he attacked.

His claws flashed in the midday sun, his tail whipped through the air, his fangs tore through flesh, bone and darkness alike.

He ripped through them, shredding their bodies, breaking their bones, scattering the cursed shadows holding them together.

It was brutal. Unrelenting. Each movement was instinct, survival, rage, grief. Each blow was a strike against something he couldn't fix. He knew these people. They had smiled at him once. They had cared for him.

And now?

He was tearing them apart.

Prak's roar split the air, shaking the very trees.

Then, it was over. The last of the shadow-covered corpses crumpled, the darkness around them withering like a dying flame.

Prak stood, his chest heaving, his claws dripping with dark, sticky ichor. He wiped his mouth with the back of his hand, his muscles shaking with exhaustion. His ears twitched. The only thing he could hear was the wind moving through the trees. No growls. No shuffling footsteps.

He was alone.

His eyes snapped toward Wilberforce's grave. Still untouched. But Esme?

Gone.

Prak's hands curled into fists, his claws digging into his palms. Atiba.

Gone.

A slow, heavy breath escaped him. Then, Prak tilted his head back and let out a long, sorrowful howl. The sound echoed throughout the village, carrying with it loss, fury, exhaustion, and grief.

His cousin was gone. Esme was back and had done the unforgivable. And Wilberforce?

Wilberforce had left him with a legacy of guardianships he never asked for. And a battle he wasn't sure he could win.

# CHAPTER 8 - ATIBA

Atiba's world dissolved into darkness.

The shadowy sludge swallowed him whole, pulling him down into a void that was neither solid nor liquid, but something in between. It was cold, so cold it burned, and thick, like tar clinging to his skin. He thrashed wildly, his arms flailing, his legs kicking, but there was nothing to grab onto, no surface to push against. The darkness pressed in on him from all sides, suffocating him, crushing him.

He tried to scream, but no sound came out. The sludge filled his mouth, his nose, his lungs. It was alive, pulsing with a rhythm that felt alien and wrong. The constellations he had seen in the shadowy tendrils earlier flickered around him, swirling like distant stars in a night sky gone mad. They were beautiful and terrifying all at once, their light cold and unfeeling.

Atiba's chest burned. His vision blurred. His body felt heavy, like it was being pulled apart and compressed at the same time. He couldn't breathe. He couldn't think. The darkness was everywhere, inside him, around him, consuming him.

This wasn't just a void. It was alive. And it didn't want him here. The realization hit him like a punch to the gut. The shadow realm wasn't just a place—it was a living, breathing thing. And he was an intruder, a foreign object, something it was trying to expel. The sludge churned violently, the constellations swirling faster, their light growing brighter, harsher. Atiba felt himself being pushed, pulled, twisted, as if the very fabric of this place was trying to tear him apart.

His struggles grew weaker. His limbs felt like lead. His vision darkened at the edges, the stars blurring into streaks of light. He was losing consciousness. He could feel it slipping away, the panic fading into a strange, numb acceptance.

Then… pain.

A sharp, electric jolt shot through his wrist, radiating up his arm and through his entire body. The bangle. It was glowing, its dull wood now alive with a faint, green light. The sludge recoiled, the constellations flickering erratically, as if startled. Atiba gasped, his lungs filling with air for the first time in what felt like an eternity.

And then, just as suddenly as it had swallowed him, the darkness spat him out.

Atiba hit the ground hard, his knees buckling beneath him. He coughed, his body trembling as he tried to catch his breath. The air was different here, colder, heavier, tinged with a metallic taste that made his tongue feel dry.

He looked around, his heart pounding in his chest. He was in the cemetery.

But it wasn't the cemetery he had just left.

The headstones were the same, their weathered surfaces familiar, but the world around them was… wrong. The colors were muted, washed out, everything cast in hues of purple and gray. The sky above was a deep, swirling indigo, devoid of stars or clouds, just an endless expanse of shifting darkness. The trees that bordered the graveyard were twisted, their branches gnarled and reaching like skeletal fingers. The air was thick with the scent of damp earth and something else, something sharp and acrid, like burnt metal.

Atiba staggered to his feet, his legs unsteady beneath him. His thoughts tumbled in a frantic jumble, trying to make sense of what had just happened. Esme. The shadowy sludge. The bangle. The words she had said: You's de new Papa Bois. What did that even mean? And who was she?

Someone who had known Wilberforce, someone who had called him an enemy. But why had she done this? Why had she sent him here?

He didn't have time to think about it. A low moan broke the silence.

Atiba froze. The sound came from behind him, from one of the graves. He turned slowly, his heart pounding in his chest.

The ground was moving. The dirt shifted, rising and falling like the surface of a restless sea. Then, with a sickening crunch, a hand burst through the soil, pale, skeletal, its fingers clawing at the air. Another hand followed, then another, and another. The graves were opening, the earth splitting apart as figures began to emerge.

Jumbies.

Atiba had heard the stories, of course. Whenever he returned home after midnight, his mother would always force him back out unless he walked through the front door backwards.

"Doh bring no jumbie in my house, nah!" she'd say. He'd always swear under his breath and acquiesce, thinking it to be nothing more than silly superstition, but…

But now… seeing them, watching as they rose from their graves, their forms shimmering like smoke and shadow, their eyes burning with an unnatural light, was something else entirely.

These weren't just corpses. They were wraiths: ethereal, malevolent, and ravenous. Their bodies were insubstantial, flickering between solidity and shadow, as if they existed in two worlds at once. Their edges blurred, trailing wisps of darkness that dissolved into the air like ink in water. Their eyes glowed with a cold, pale light, piercing through the gloom, and their mouths hung open in silent, eternal screams. The air around them rippled with heat, a sudden, oppressive warmth that made Atiba's skin prickle and his head swim. He felt disoriented, his vision blurring as the jumbies drew closer, their ghostly forms shifting and writhing like flames in the wind.

He didn't wait to see what they would do. He ran.

The jumbies' moans followed him, filled with a hunger that made his skin crawl. He refused to look back. His legs carried him forward, his feet pounding against the dirt path as he fled the cemetery. The village was ahead—or at least, the shadowy version of it. He could see the outlines of houses in the distance, their shapes distorted, their colors muted. But he didn't make it that far.

A forest closed in around him.

It wasn't the same forest he had seen on the way back to Boisdepin, where he'd seen that mysterious child. This one was denser, darker, the trees towering overhead, their branches intertwined to form a canopy that blocked out what little light there was. The underbrush was thick, the ground uneven, littered with roots and rocks that seemed to reach out to trip him.

Atiba's legs burned as he tore through the shadowy forest and and he sucked in air that never seemed to reach his lungs. The jumbies—or whatever they were—were close. Too close. Their moans echoed through the trees, a haunting chorus that sent shivers down his spine. He could feel their presence behind him, the oppressive heat they radiated making the air thick and heavy. His head swam, his vision blurring as he stumbled over roots and rocks, the forest seeming to conspire against him.

Thorny vines snagged his clothes, their sharp barbs tearing at his skin. Low-hanging branches whipped against his face, leaving stinging welts. His feet slipped on moss-covered rocks, sending him sprawling more than once. Each fall left him more battered, more desperate, but he couldn't stop.

The jumbies were relentless.

Their moans grew louder, more frantic, their hunger palpable. Atiba didn't dare look back. His only thought was to keep moving, to put as much distance between himself and them as possible.

And then, he heard it.

A shrill, spine-tingling whistle pierced the air, cutting through the jumbies' voices like a knife. Atiba stumbled to a halt, his chest thrummed with panicked beats. The sound was unnatural, otherworldly, and it sent a chill down his spine. He looked around, his eyes scanning the forest, but he saw nothing.

Then, he felt it. A presence.

It was immense, towering, and it radiated a cold, ancient power that made the jumbies' heat seem like a warm breeze in comparison. Atiba's breath caught in his throat as he slowly turned, his eyes widening in horror.

There, standing in the middle of the path, was… something.

At first, he thought it was a tree—two massive, gnarled trunks rising from the ground, their surfaces rough and weathered. But as he stepped closer, his heart sank. Those weren't trees. They were legs. Impossibly tall, impossibly thick, they stretched up into the sky, their owner's body looming in the shadows above.

What the hell was this thing? Atiba stared up at it incredulously. It wasn't human—not even close. Its legs were spread wide, straddling the road, its massive feet planted firmly on the ground. Its body was thin and elongated, its arms hanging limply at its sides. Its head was tilted back, its face obscured by the shadows, but Atiba could feel its gaze fixed on something above—the moon, maybe?

The jumbies stopped. Their moans faded into silence as they hesitated, their glowing eyes flickering with fear. Even they knew better than to cross this… thing.

Atiba's pulse thundered in his ears as he looked at the creature. He couldn't go back. The jumbies were behind him, their heat pressing in on him. He couldn't go forward. This thing blocked the path, its presence overwhelming.

Think. Think.

He didn't know what it was, but he knew he didn't want to find out what would happen if he tried to pass under it. Slowly, carefully, he moved.

He stepped off the path, his feet sinking into the soft, damp earth. The creature didn't move, its gaze still fixed on the moon. A wild rhythm hammered through him as he crept around it, his eyes never leaving its massive form.

The jumbies watched from a distance, their glowing eyes flickering with unease. They didn't follow. They didn't dare.

Breath tore in and out of him as he moved, his body trembling with fear and exhaustion. Every step felt like an eternity, every sound: the rustle of leaves, the crunch of twigs, like a thunderclap in the silence.

And then, he was past it.

The creature remained still, its gaze fixed on the moon, its presence fading into the shadows. He ran, his legs carrying him deeper into the forest, away from the jumbies, away from the towering monstrosity, away from the nightmare he had just escaped.

But the forest wasn't done with him.

Tree limbs arched over him, a warped cathedral of bark and leaves. The underbrush was thick, the ground uneven, littered with roots and rocks that seemed to reach out to trip him. Atiba stumbled, his foot catching on a root. He fell hard, his hands scraping against the rough bark of a fallen log. Pain shot through his palms, but he didn't have time to stop. He pushed himself up and kept running, each inhale scraping his throat raw.

The jumbies' wails rolled through the trees like distant sirens, a haunting reminder that they were still out there, still hunting him. He didn't know where he was going. He didn't know if there was anywhere to go. All he knew was that he had to keep running.

And then, just as he thought he couldn't go any further, he saw it. A clearing.

The trees thinned ahead, the underbrush giving way to open space. Atiba pushed himself harder, his legs screaming in protest as he sprinted toward it. The jumbies were close. So close he could almost feel their cold, decaying hands reaching for him.

He burst into the clearing, his chest heaving, his body trembling with exhaustion.

And then he stopped. Because the jumbies were gone.

The moans had faded, the oppressive heat had vanished. The clearing was silent, the air cool and still. Atiba scanned the trees for any sign of the creatures. But they were gone. For now, at least, he was safe.

He allowed himself a moment to catch his breath, his hands resting on his knees as he tried to steady himself. But as he straightened up, his eyes caught movement in the trees.

At first, he thought it was a trick of the light. A shadow shifting, a branch swaying. But then he saw it again. And again. And again.

Children.

They were perched in the trees, their small forms barely visible in the dim light. Atiba gulped when he realized what he was seeing. It was the child from the road, the one who had stolen his phone. And there were more.

Dozens of them, their small bodies crouched on branches, their faces hidden beneath large, floppy straw hats.

Then they began to move.

They scurried down the tree trunks with unnatural speed, their movements jerky and erratic. Within seconds, they had surrounded him, their small forms closing in from all sides. He took a step back, his eyes darting between them.

And then he saw the details.

Their feet were backwards, the heels facing forward, the knees bent the wrong way. Their hands were small and delicate, but their movements were quick, almost predatory. Their faces were hidden beneath their hats, but he could see their mouths. Small, round openings that seemed to twitch and shift as if they were whispering to each other.

Thoughts crashed over each other, useless and panicked. What were these things? They weren't children... not real ones, anyway. They were something else. Something... wrong.

One of them stepped forward, its head tilting slightly as if studying him. Its mouth opened, and a voice came out, soft, melodic, and eerily familiar.

"Atiba..."

It was his mother's voice.

Atiba's blood ran cold. He took a step back. "Stay back," he said, his voice trembling.

The creature tilted its head again, its mouth twitching. "Atiba..." it said again, the voice shifting now, becoming deeper, more masculine. It was his father's voice: a man he hadn't heard speak in years.

The young man clenched his hands into fists, his body trembling with fear and anger. "Stop it," he said, his voice louder now. "Whatever you are, just… stop."

The creatures didn't move. They just stood there, their small forms silent and still. And then, as if on some unseen signal, they began to close in.

They scuttled forward, their small, twisted forms moving with eerie precision. Their backwards feet shuffled across the forest floor, their floppy straw hats hiding their faceless heads, their small mouths twitching as they whispered his name in voices that weren't their own. He backed up until he hit a tree, his chest heaving, his mind racing. There was no way out. No escape. He was surrounded.

He closed his eyes, bracing himself for whatever came next. The whispers grew louder, more insistent, the coldness of their presence pressing in on him. He could feel them closing in, their small hands reaching for him.

But then… nothing.

The whispers stopped. The cold faded. Sound leaked out of the world, leaving only the thud of his pulse.

Atiba's breath hitched. He waited, his body tense, his eyes still shut tight. But nothing happened.

No hands grabbed him. No teeth sank into his flesh. Just… silence. Cautiously, he opened his eyes.

And there, standing between him and the creatures, was a man.

Atiba blinked, his mind struggling to process what he was seeing. The man was slightly taller than him, his frame broad and muscular, his posture relaxed but ready. He was barefoot, wearing a simple gray tracksuit that clung to his powerful build. His hair was styled in a fauxhawk, the tail tied up in the back, and his light bronze skin glistened faintly in the dim light.

Atiba couldn't see his face, he was staring at the man's broad, muscular back, but there was something familiar about him.

The children were no longer advancing. Instead, they hovered at a distance, their small forms shifting uneasily, their whispers fading into silence. They seemed… scared.

The man half-turned his head, glancing back at Atiba. His face was sharp, his features stern, his dark eyes piercing. And then it clicked. This was the surly teen from that one photograph back at his grandfather's house. The one who had been standing next to Prak, his arms crossed, his expression annoyed. But he wasn't a teen anymore. He was a man now, his presence commanding, his aura radiating a quiet, dangerous power.

"When dey fall back," the man said, his voice low and steady, his Trinidadian accent thick, "yuh run. If yuh want to survive dis place, yuh follow me. Understand?"

Atiba just nodded. Arguing cost energy he didn't have. "Yeah," he said, his voice barely above a whisper.

His savior turned back toward the Douen, his posture shifting slightly, his muscles tensing. The creatures hissed, their small mouths twitching, but they didn't move. They just stood there, their backwards feet shuffling nervously.

And then he let out a loud, guttural yell.

The sound echoed through the forest, sharp and primal, and the child-like creatures recoiled, their small forms jerking back as if struck. Atiba's eyes widened as tendrils of shadow erupted from the other man's body, lashing out toward the creatures like whips. The shadows struck with precision, each one hitting its mark, sending them scrambling back into the trees.

The man didn't wait. He turned on his heel, his movements fluid and precise, and grabbed Atiba firmly by the arm. "Move," he said, his voice firm but not unkind.

The young man didn't argue. He let the older man pull him along, his legs moving almost on their own as they dashed deeper into the forest. The trees blurred around them, the ground uneven and treacherous, but the man moved with a confidence that suggested he knew this place well.

Who was this guy? Why had he stepped in? And what the hell was going on? But there was no time to ask questions. The Douen were behind them, their whispers growing louder, their coldness pressing in on them again.

The man ran, his grip on Atiba's arm firm but not painful. Atiba followed, his body aching, his lungs burning, but he didn't stop. He couldn't.

And then, just as he thought he couldn't go any further, the man pulled him into a small, hidden alcove beneath the roots of a massive tree. He pushed Atiba down, his hand firm but not rough, and crouched beside him, his eyes scanning the forest.

"Stay quiet," the man whispered, his voice barely audible. "Dey cyah find we here."

Atiba nodded, his breath coming in shallow gasps. He pressed himself against the tree root. The whispers grew louder, but the Douen didn't come closer. They lingered at the edge of the alcove, their small forms shifting uneasily.

And then, they were gone.

The forest fell silent, the cold fading, the whispers disappearing into the shadows. Atiba let out a shaky breath, his body trembling with exhaustion and relief.

His rescuer turned to him, his dark eyes studying him carefully. "Yuh alright?" he asked, his voice low, carrying the weight of someone who already knew the answer.

Atiba nodded, though his chest still heaved and his legs felt hollow. "Yeah," he rasped, though it sounded more like a question than truth. "Thanks… for that."

The man grunted, neither warm nor cold, his expression unreadable beneath the shadow of the trees. "Yuh lucky ah find yuh when ah did. Dis place eh kind to outsiders."

Atiba blinked sweat from his eyes, still trying to steady his breath. "What… what WERE those things?"

The man's gaze flicked back to the dark where the shapes had vanished. His lip curled faintly, but whether it was amusement or disdain, Atiba couldn't tell. "Douen," he said at last. "Spirits of children who dead before baptism. They wander barefoot, foot turn backward, face blank like clay… always searching, always hungry."

The word 'spirits' landed heavy in Atiba's chest. "S-spirits…?" he stammered.

"Mm." The man's voice was flat, final. "And good moves with the moon gazer too."

Atiba frowned, confused. "Moon… gazer…?"

The man's eyes narrowed, watching him as though to weigh whether he was truly so ignorant. "That tall thing yuh see," he said, lifting a hand to mimic the giant's height. "Long legs, head in the clouds. If yuh did pass between he legs, boy…" His teeth clicked once, sharp in the quiet. "Yuh woulda been mashed to paste."

Atiba's throat worked as he swallowed, dry as sand. His thoughts spun back to that path flanked by those towering, tree-like limbs, the one even the other jumbies refused to go near. A shiver crawled down his spine as he realized how close he had come.

He licked his lips, hesitated, then asked, "Wait… how did you know I saw the moon gazer?"

The man's gaze cut back to him, steady, unreadable. "Cause ah been trailin' yuh. Waitin' fuh de right time to step in. Ah could take jumbies, but ah eh too eager to fight them in packs."

Relief and unease tangled inside the young man. Whoever this guy was, he hadn't just saved his life—he'd been watching him long before this moment.

Atiba's voice cracked as it left him. "Who… who are you?"

The older man hesitated for a moment, his dark eyes narrowing as he studied Atiba. He didn't offer his name, only gestured for Atiba to follow. "Come on," he said, his voice low and steady. "We need to keep movin'."

Atiba nodded, too tired and overwhelmed to argue. He followed the man as they moved deeper into the forest, the oppressive darkness of the shadow world gradually giving way to something... different. The air grew lighter, the colors brighter, the oppressive purple hue fading into softer, more natural tones. The trees seemed less twisted here, their branches arching gracefully overhead, their leaves shimmering with a faint, silvery light. The ground beneath his feet felt softer, almost welcoming, as if the forest itself was guiding him forward.

As they walked, Atiba's mind was full of questions. He glanced at the man, his curiosity outweighing his caution. "Who are you?" he asked again, his voice barely above a whisper.

The other man didn't answer immediately. He kept his gaze forward, his expression unreadable. Finally, as they approached the edge of a clearing, he stopped and turned to Atiba. "Jumbies don't have names," he said simply, his tone matter-of-fact but carrying a weight of unspoken history. Before he could process the fact that he identified himself as a Jumbie, the man continued. "Now, stay close. And don't speak unless she speaks to you first."

Atiba blinked, his mouth opening to ask more, but the man was already stepping into the clearing. Atiba followed, his breath catching in his throat as he took in the sight before him.

The clearing was unlike anything he had ever seen. A small waterfall cascaded down a rocky outcrop, its crystal-clear waters shimmering as they flowed into a serpentine river that wound through the trees. The air smelled fresh, tinged with the crisp scent of damp earth and something faintly sweet, like ripened fruit just before it fell from the tree. Flowers bloomed along the riverbank, their colors impossibly vivid, untouched by decay or shadow. The light here was… softer. Not quite like daylight, nor moonlight, but something in-between a gentle radiance that seemed to hum against his skin.

The sounds of the jungle returned, but not as they had been in the forest outside of Boisdepin. No cicadas droned. No distant roosters crowed. No wind howled through the trees. Instead, there was music. Not the kind made by instruments, but a natural symphony: the rush of the river, the chirping of unseen birds, the rustling of leaves, all perfectly balanced, as if orchestrated by some unseen force.

Atiba's eyes were drawn to the river, where a figure perched on a smooth rock at the water's edge.

She was beautiful. Her long, dark hair cascaded down her back in luminous waves, her chocolate skin glowing with an otherworldly light. But it wasn't just her presence. It was the way the world bent around her, like she belonged to it in a way he never could. The air seemed to shimmer in her presence, the light bending and refracting as if paying homage to her.

She was both part of the landscape and something beyond it, her very existence defying the natural order.

Then his gaze traveled downward. And his stomach clenched.

Where her legs should have been, long, sinuous coils gleamed in the dim light—shimmering, iridescent scales reflecting the hues of the water. They shifted subtly as she moved, the scales catching the light in a mesmerizing dance of color and shadow.

Atiba's lungs tightened.

A mermaid? No. Not a mermaid. Something else. Something… older.

The man stepped forward, his posture relaxed but respectful. He dipped his head slightly, his voice calm but carrying a weight of reverence. "Mama D'leau," he said. "Ah bring him. Like you wanted."

# CHAPTER 9 - ESME

The air was heavy.

Not with heat or humidity, but with *consequence*.

Esme stood alone in the vast emptiness of the East Gates Mall parking lot, bathed in the pallid fluorescence of overhead lights that flickered as if straining to stay awake. The hour was neither night nor morning, the kind of time when the world thinned and it felt like the past and future could both seep through the cracks of now.

She had never actually been to this mall before. East Gates was new, polished, almost too pristine. But Trincity Mall, just down the road, had been her real haunt, the place she and her friends once claimed like their own kingdom. Saturdays blurred into late afternoons, the clatter of food court trays, the scent of fried chicken and soft-serve, the thrill of buying nothing yet feeling rich just being there. On weekdays, when they cut class and slipped through the sliding doors, the mall became their refuge.

For her friends, those stolen hours were rebellion, laughter, and lightness. For her, they were borrowed time. The last carefree days before she had to shoulder the weight her caretakers pressed onto her shoulders. Before her name became something whispered, and her mask became something feared.

She shifted on her heels, arms wrapped tightly across her chest as if shielding herself from the cold. There was no breeze, but the silence clung to her like mist. Her clothes still smelled faintly of earth and ash from the cemetery, from her conjured dead, from the violence she had wrought.

She had done it.

She had traded Atiba's life for Levi's.

And yet, the triumph she had expected never came.

Instead, her mind was choked with memories. Atiba's voice, small and confused, cried for help as the ground swallowed him. Prak's howl of anguish as he stood among the ruined dead.

That sound had pierced something in her. It still echoed, haunting the spaces between her breaths.

She hadn't wanted it to go that far. She hadn't wanted to hurt him. Prak, the shy, anxious teenager who used to trail behind Levi like a shadow, barely speaking above a whisper. She had been the one to coax him out of his shell, the one who helped him find language for the storm inside him when his powers began to spiral out of control. Back then, she'd been more than just a friend. She'd been his lifeline. But now, he'd gotten in the way. And she couldn't afford sentiment.

Not when Levi was so close. Not when this was the only way.

Still... she hated the way he'd looked at her. A soft whoosh of air shifted her attention.

Headlights crept over the horizon like a pair of predatory eyes. A long, black limousine pulled into view, tires whispering over the asphalt as it glided toward her. The engine made no sound, like it was floating instead of driving. Her heart clenched when she saw the license plate: 333

The limo rolled to a stop beside her, and a moment later, the back door opened. From within stepped Ms. Millicent, elegant as ever, her gray suit crisp and unwrinkled despite the hour. Beside her was Heartmann, looking like a wolf wearing a man's skin. His smug expression hadn't shifted since the day they met. He was still grinning, like the punchline of a joke only he knew was coming.

Millicent nodded. "Have you completed your task?"

Esme didn't answer right away. She looked past them to the open door of the limo. Darkness pooled inside like ink; an invitation laced with danger.

She swallowed. "Yes."

Millicent's expression didn't change. "Then enter. Mr. Brown is waiting."

A flicker of instinct flared in her chest, don't trust them. But she smothered it. She had come too far to back out now.

Still, she didn't move immediately. "If this is a setup…" she warned, her voice low.

Millicent cut in smoothly. "You'll know shortly."

Heartmann laughed.

Esme rolled her eyes, then drew a breath. She could take them if she had to. Or melt into the shadows before they could blink. Her ability, her birthright, made her impossible to cage. Even if the thought of using the shadows in that particular way made her shudder.

She stepped into the limo.

The door clicked shut behind her, sealing her in with an oppressive silence that smelled of crushed myrrh and something faintly metallic… blood?

No… something older. Like rust on the spine of time.

The space inside was dim, backlit by a single golden bar light casting soft, warm glows across crystal decanters. The scent in the limo wasn't just incense. It was aged paper, musk, a trace of ozone, like a storm had passed through a library.

He sat directly across from her.

A man. Immaculately dressed. A black suit, tailored so finely it looked grown on him, not sewn. A silver pocket square, folded with surgical precision, peeked from his breast pocket. His skin was smooth, deep bronze. Too flawless to be ordinary. His dreadlocks were shoulder-length, streaked with hints of silver at the temples, and pulled back loosely behind his head. His beard was short, refined, not a hair out of place. He wore no jewelry, save for a single onyx ring shaped like a crow's beak on his left index finger.

He wore custom glasses with mismatched lenses, one black, opaque as midnight, and the other clear as crystal, giving him the disquieting impression that he could see into both light and shadow at once.

His one visible eye was arresting: wide, warm brown, but ancient. Bottomless. It gave the impression of knowing not just who you were, but who you had been. Who you almost became.

"Esme," he said, his voice laced in a Jamaican accent, smooth and melodic. There was no slang, no laziness in his speech. Every word was intentional. Measured. Almost ceremonial. "It's a pleasure to finally speak."

He gestured toward the built-in bar to his left. "May I offer you a drink? Whisky? Rum? Something sweet, perhaps?"

She didn't move. "No. I'm good."

He smiled gently.

"Of course. Business first, then."

Her jaw tightened.

"You know why I'm here."

Instead of answering, he leaned forward slightly and plucked a glass from the bar. He poured himself something dark and amber, swirled it gently, then sipped, but didn't swallow. It sat in his mouth a moment, as though being tasted for memory, not flavor.

"You ever think about what we lose every day?" he asked suddenly. "Not people. Not things. Culture. Tongue. Rhythm. Names."

Esme narrowed her eyes. "What?"

"Once," he said, his gaze drifting to the dark window, "there was a people who could call storms with their drums. Who could walk in both worlds, living and dead, without fear. Then came enslavement. Then came relocation. Then came silence. Civilization. Concrete."

Mr. Brown's eyes lingered on her, their warmth veiling a kind of ancient scrutiny. When he finally spoke, it was in that same gentle, melodic Jamaican cadence. Measured, hypnotic, almost too smooth.

"You ever think about what it means to be descended from pain?" he asked, swirling the amber liquid in his glass. "Not just touched by it. Not wounded by it. But built from it. Shaped by a legacy handed down, like a rusty cutlass passed from trembling hand to trembling hand."

Esme didn't respond at first. The hum of the limo was the only sound between them. She kept her arms crossed, her jaw tight.

"I think about what I have to do to survive," she said finally, her voice low. "Not what caused the problem."

He smiled slightly. "And yet, the problem started long before the Day of Darkness seven years ago. Long before you. Long before your brothers." His gaze flicked toward the shadows at her feet. "Even before your mother. Or hers."

Esme's spine stiffened.

"You've met her, haven't you? Or at least the shell of the woman she eventually became," he added. "Your living, ancient ancestor, I mean. Tanty, I believe you all called her. A woman of deep will. Deep hurt."

Esme's breath caught in her throat. "You know about Tanty?"

"I know enough," he said, calmly. "I know she stood at the edge of the cane fields and whispered words not meant for men to hear. That she called on old blood, older than the British flag, older than chains. And that in her wrath, she bent a curse around the necks of those who betrayed her."

Esme felt her mouth go dry.

Mr. Brown leaned forward, his voice still gentle.

"The Porter family. They thought they could touch her. Use her. And discard her like soursop skin.

But she was not the kind of woman you discard."

"She destroyed them," Esme whispered, more to herself than to him.

"No," he corrected softly. "You did. She simply set the tide and used you as her instrument. The storm was always going to come. You were just the thunder."

Esme shook her head slowly. "I didn't ask for any of this. Neither did Levi. Or Darren."

"And yet here you are," Mr. Brown said, not unkindly. "Carrying a power older than your language. A power that doesn't forget. One your ancestor called into being when she tore open the veil and demanded the land remember her."

Esme's fingers twitched. Her shadow pulsed faintly against the limo floor.

Mr. Brown reclined, looking utterly at ease. "Tell me, Esme… how many generations of Porters suffered because of her curse? How many lived long enough to rot in guilt? And how many were born warped by it—born wrong, like fruit spoiled on the vine?"

Her throat clenched. "What does that have to do with me?"

"Everything," he said, finishing his drink. "In her desperation to regain even just a fragment of her once mighty power, she orchestrated your creation… a Porter child born of her own bloodline."

He gave Esme a fatherly smile, so innocent and unassuming it rattled her. "You, Esme, carry both the wound and the blade," he continued, "And only you can decide which one you'll use."

She stared at him, not blinking. "That's not a choice. That's manipulation."

"It's history," he replied evenly. "I'm just reminding you of it."

"And why do you care?" she snapped. "You talk like you were there. Like you watched her curse them."

"I did."

Esme stared.

Mr. Brown only smiled, his eyes unreadable. "And I've seen what happens when old wounds fester in the dark. When the stories die. When guardians like Wilberforce silence what needs to be heard."

Her breath trembled in her chest. "Wilberforce protected people."

He nodded slowly. "Yes. He built walls. Strong ones. But walls don't only keep danger out. They keep truth in. And now you've pulled one down."

Esme's voice dropped to a whisper. "So what now? The world burns?"

"No." Mr. Brown's voice was soft. "The world remembers. You remember. That's the first step."

There was a long silence between them. Then his gaze sharpened.

"And now, the bargain," he said. Her pulse spiked.

"I no longer sense Papa Bois. You've done well."

She wet her lips, her mouth suddenly dry. "Why?" she asked. "Why did he have to die?"

Mr. Brown tapped a single finger on the rim of his glass. "Because he was the last breath of an old era. The heir of a man who mistook stewardship for dominion. Who believed the land could only be protected by his hands, his rules. There is no place for such rigidity in what's coming."

"And what's coming?" she asked, her voice sharp.

He ignored the question. "You removed the lock from the gate. Now, the forest—and everything tied to it—can begin again. New roots. New stories. Not his."

She shook her head slowly. "You talk like this was some holy mission." "It is survival," he said simply. "For you. For Levi. For the others like you. And for those who will never be like you."

Esme leaned forward now. "Speaking of Levi… you said you could bring him back."

"I said he could be helped," Mr. Brown corrected. "And he can."

"How?"

"You already have what you need." His eyes flicked briefly to her shadow. "Your gift allows you to traverse the threshold. That dark place… that void you can and Levi once could access by using your shadows as a portal… it's not the end. It's the in-between. The hallway between the house of the living and the ruins of the dead. When he died, Levi never made it through. His spirit clung to the seam."

Her lips parted. "So, he's there."

"He's waiting," Mr. Brown said. "But the further you go, the harder it is to return. That's the cost of crossing."

Her hands curled into fists. "Why didn't you just tell me all this before?"

He smiled faintly. "Because you wouldn't have been willing to pay the price. Not until now."

Before she could speak again, Mr. Brown rapped once on the glass. The car slowed.

"We're here," he said softly.

The door opened beside her. Cool air spilled in, the faint sound of birds beginning to chirp somewhere in the waking distance.

Esme hesitated. "That's it?"

"You asked for Levi," he said. "Now go find him."

She stepped out slowly, the shadows at her feet stretching long and thick beneath her. The door closed behind her. The limo drifted away into the pre-dawn mist, its red taillights swallowed by the fog like embers dying in water.

Alone now, Esme stared down at the shadows swirling around her feet—once silent, once obedient.

But now? Now they shifted. Whispered. Beckoned.

And for the first time, she wasn't sure if they were following her…

…or leading her somewhere she could never come back from.

She wrapped her arms around herself, suddenly aware of how cold the air had become. The parking lot was empty, but she kept looking over her shoulder, half-expecting Mr. Brown to still be there, watching her with that quiet, all-knowing smile.

Her pulse quickened. Her thoughts churned. He said he was there.

There when Tanty had cursed the Porter family. There when the ancient bonds were forged.

He said it like it was yesterday. Like he'd watched it happen. But that was impossible.

Tanty's curse was centuries old… older than memory, older than the village, older than the country itself. The only beings who could have endured that long were Papa Bois and Tanty herself, sustained by her pact with the spirits. Even Esme, who had grown up in the shadows of those stories, hadn't known the full truth until her mother told her. So how had this man known?

How had he known her ancestor? Her lineage?

The secrets even the rest of her family never dared speak aloud? He had to be lying. Had to be.

Maybe he'd stolen the knowledge from some old obeahman, or maybe Millicent had access to records Esme didn't know about. Maybe there was surveillance. A mole in the family. Something, anything— But even as the rationalizations formed, they fell apart. Because deep down, she'd felt it.

That chilling, ageless presence in the backseat of the limo. That impossible gravity in his voice. She'd tried to meet his gaze and found herself staring into something older than time, something that had never known sleep, never known silence. There had been no pretense. No façade.

Exactly as it had been the first time, she met Wilberforce. He hadn't been lying.

And now, standing in the middle of an empty parking lot at the edge of dawn, Esme realized a truth that froze her deeper than any shadow ever had. She didn't know who—or what—Mr. Brown really was, but she knew this much: She'd just helped him remove the one person who could have stopped whatever he had planned.

What exactly had she set into motion?

Her eyes drifted back to the shifting darkness around her feet. They still moved under her will. Still waited for her command. Still bent to her touch, the way Levi's once had.

But there was one thing she couldn't do. Couldn't make herself do. Enter them.

The shadow realm—the in-between, the liminal corridor between the living and the dead—was hers to command. She could summon it at will, pull its veil into the world of flesh and bone, drape it over herself and others, shape it into armor, blades, whispers that cut deeper than steel.

But she would not step inside it. Not because she couldn't. Not because of some hidden flaw in the gift.

Because that was where she had laid Levi's body. Her last act of mourning. Her penance. Her promise.

She had never crossed that threshold again.

And now, the shadows whispered, asking her to. For Levi.

# CHAPTER 10 - PRAK

The roar that had split the cemetery faded into nothing, leaving only Prak's ragged breath and the faint hiss of flies gathering over what he had torn apart. His claws were still dripping shadow-ichor when the weight of it hit him all at once, the stillness, the emptiness, the absence. His body ached. His soul ached more.

He staggered out of the cemetery and into the road, the wind cutting against his sweat. His form was still half-shifted, claws too long, eyes glowing faintly, his jaw unhinged enough to bare fangs. He caught his reflection in the car window and snarled, disgust rising in his throat.

If the villagers saw him like this, they would not see Prak, grandson of Wilberforce. They would see a beast.

With a groan, he forced it down. His claws retracted, painful and slow, until his fingers looked human again. His jaw snapped back into place, leaving a dull throb in his skull. His glowing eyes dimmed to brown, though the pupils still pulsed sharp as a cat's. By the time he reached the edge of Boisdepin proper, he looked like a man again, ragged, sweat-stained, but a man.

Even so, he couldn't hide the weight in his stride. "Evening, Prak!" someone called from a veranda. He didn't answer.

A group of children raced past, one shouting his name with glee. Normally he would have ruffled their heads, growled a half-joking threat to chase them off. Now he kept walking, eyes straight, as if their voices couldn't touch him.

He heard the concern in whispers trailing behind him. "What wrong with he?" "He look like ghost." "Something happen at de cemetery?"

He ignored them all. His legs moved on instinct, carrying him past familiar shops, past Wilberforce's old haunts, past neighbors who had known him since boyhood. None of it touched him.

His feet carried him, as they always did, back home.

Wilberforce's house. Now Atiba's house.

The door creaked as he pushed it open. Inside, the air was stale, still heavy with Wilberforce's scent of cedar and old tobacco, but undercut now with dust. He didn't light a lamp. Shadows filled the corners.

He dropped into Wilberforce's armchair, the old one that had cradled the weight of the elder for decades. The cushions sighed under him, as if they too knew who was missing.

The wall of photographs stared down. Generations of Boisdepin. Faces faded by time but still proud, still fixed in stiff suits and dresses, frozen in their Sunday best. His eyes drifted from frame to frame until they caught the last picture he had taken with Wilberforce.

The old man's hand had been heavy on his shoulder. His smile steady, proud. The kind of smile that said, You'll carry this when I'm gone.

Prak's throat burned. His fingers dug into the chair arms.

"You were wrong, old man," he muttered. His voice was hoarse, almost breaking. "Ah wasn't good enough. Not to be Papa Bois. Not even to guide the one who is."

His jaw trembled.

And worse… Atiba. His cousin. His blood. The one Wilberforce had trusted fate to. Gone.

Prak leaned forward, elbows on his knees, his face in his hands. He dragged his fingers down until they pressed against his lips, muffling the words.

"What ah go tell his mother?"

Prak's chest shook with the weight of it. He saw her face, heard her voice, imagined her saying the words: You were supposed to watch him. You were supposed to keep him safe.

And he had failed.

He pressed his forehead into his palms and let out a low, broken sound. Not quite a growl, not quite a sob… something caught in the middle, raw and unshaped.

For a long while, he sat there. The house groaned softly with the night. The photographs stared. The air pressed heavier and heavier until he thought it might suffocate him.

Then it hit. A pressure in his chest.

Prak jerked upright, claws half-sprung before he realized he wasn't in danger. The sensation came again, quick, sharp, wrong. His breath caught.

Fear. Not his.

It sliced through his ribs like a cold blade, stealing the air from his lungs. His heart stuttered, pounding in his ears, and for a wild moment he thought it was a panic attack. But no. He had known fear. This wasn't his.

It pulsed again, sharper, and his throat tightened as if invisible hands were choking him. His breath rasped. His skin crawled.

Then he knew.

"Atiba," he whispered, voice breaking.

The fear came clearer now, threading itself into his own heartbeat. It was raw. Naked. Terrified. The kind of fear only blood could carry across worlds. Prak staggered out of the chair, hands clutching the armrests until the old wood creaked. His chest heaved.

"Atiba… yuh alive."

He stood there in the half-dark, the photographs staring down, his grandfather's shadow heavy over him, and for the first time since Wilberforce's death, Prak felt the tug of something larger than himself.

A call. A warning. A chance. And he would answer.

The truth pressed down on him like the old armchair cushions, heavy, suffocating. He didn't know what had happened in that cemetery, but Esme had done something to Atiba. Taken him. Somewhere beyond the veil. And if Atiba's terror could bleed into him… then the veil wasn't holding.

His jaw clenched.

He thought of Atiba's mother. He didn't know her well… only that she had stayed in Queens when Wilberforce died, too proud or too bitter to come home for the funeral. She and her father had never seen eye to eye, and it was clear that tension had bled into her relationship with her son. Coldness passed down like an heirloom.

Prak had judged her for it. Still did. But even so… even someone that callous, someone who could ignore her father's death and rush to sell off his life's work, even she would feel something if her boy simply vanished. If he never called again. If he never came back.

Prak's stomach twisted. He could picture her face if the news ever reached her. Or worse, if no news reached her at all, and Atiba just became another silence in her life.

"No," he muttered, fists curling tight. "Ah not losing him. Not like this."

Prak shoved away from the window, snatched his grandfather's old cutlass from its place above the door, and stalked into the night.

The villagers called to him again as he passed, their greetings nervous but insistent. He ignored them all. His pace quickened, his feet carrying him past the edge of the village, past the yam patches and coconut trees, into the thick belly of the forest.

# CHAPTER 11 - ATIBA

The woman's eyes met Atiba's, deep and dark, like the river itself, and they seemed to see straight through him. For a heartbeat she froze, her face shifting in quiet shock. Her gaze lingered on his jaw, his cheekbones, the set of his shoulders.

"Will…" she whispered under her breath, her voice trembling with memory. Then she shook her head slightly, recovering herself. "De resemblance is… striking."

She smiled, her expression warm, almost maternal. "Ah didn't expect de forest to send me de next Papa Bois so soon."

Atiba's chest tightened at the phrase. That title again.

"Welcome, child," she continued, her voice carrying both warmth and authority. "Yuh could call me Glo."

Atiba blinked. "Glo?"

She nodded, her smile widening. "Dat's right. Come, sit. Yuh look like yuh could use a rest."

He hesitated, glancing at the man, Jumbie. Gruff and unsmiling, but standing close enough to her that Atiba sensed trust.

"She safe," Jumbie said flatly, his voice carrying the kind of finality that dared anyone to doubt him.

Atiba took a deep breath and stepped forward, his legs still trembling. He sat at the riverbank, letting the cool water lap against his calves.

Without a word, Glo reached into a shallow basket beside her, pulling free a small clay dish. On it lay a simple meal, roasted fish, golden skin crisped, its bones neatly scored. She placed it gently into Atiba's hands.

"Eat," she said softly. "Yuh spirit cyah mend on emptiness."

The smell hit him first: earthy, clean, unlike the grease-slick meals back home. He broke the flesh with shaking fingers and tasted. It melted on his tongue, tender, rich, and strangely grounding. He hadn't realized how hollow he felt until that first bite filled him. Something in his chest loosened, though he couldn't have said why.

"This is…" Atiba swallowed, startled at how hungry he'd been. "It's… good."

A faint smile touched Glo's lips. "Finish."

He did, each mouthful steadying him in a way no food ever had. By the time the plate was empty, he felt rooted, as though the forest itself had settled more firmly around him.

When he glanced up, he caught Jumbie watching him. The man's head tilted, one corner of his mouth twitching like he was trying not to laugh. His eyes carried that sly, conspiratorial gleam, as if Atiba had just walked into a joke only he and Glo understood.

"What?" Atiba asked, uneasy.

Jumbie's grin widened for half a second before he gave a low chuckle and looked away, saying nothing. Glo watched in silence, her expression unreadable but warm; a gaze more motherly than anything he could remember. "Yuh been through plenty," she said softly. "But yuh safe here."

Atiba nodded weakly. "Thanks. Um… if you don't mind me asking… Who or what is Papa Bois? That woman, Esme, said my grandfather was Papa Bois. And now she's calling me his successor? I don't get it."

Glo leaned closer, her eyes shimmering with something ancient. "Papa Bois is de Father of de Woods," she said with quiet reverence. "Protector of every tree, every beast dat walk de forest. He is de healer, de guardian, de bridge between man and wild. When de world forgets to listen, he remind it. When men take too much, he restore balance."

Her smile softened, though sadness flickered beneath it. "And Wilberforce… he carried dat burden longer than most. Strong. Wise. But even he couldn't live forever."

Atiba looked down, the weight pressing against his chest. "But… why me? Prak is his grandson too. He's stronger, he knows the forest. He belongs here. Why not him?"

For the first time, Glo's expression faltered. She studied Atiba for a long moment before answering, her tone gentle. "Not all who carry de blood carry de gift. Maybe this Prak IS strong, IS dutiful. But de stag came to you, Atiba. Not to him. De forest doh just want strength. It want will. It wants heart. An' de stag sees dat in you."

Atiba blinked. "The stag…? I thought it was an elk."

A small chuckle escaped her. "Not elk, chile. Stag. Wilberforce would'a laugh if he hears you call it dat, ah sure. De stag is de essence of

Papa Bois itself. It appears to test each heir. It came to Will long ago. And now, it come to you."

Atiba swallowed hard, unable to shake the memory of its gaze burning into him.

Jumbie snorted. "So he just get chosen. Just so. Some ah we fight for every scrap of power, and he born lucky?"

Glo's gaze flicked to him, calm but firm. "Not lucky. Marked. De choice never easy, never fair. But it is de choice de forest made."

Silence lingered, heavy as the river mist.

Atiba's thoughts spun. "If that's true… then why did Esme attack me? She said it was because I was Papa Bois. But why would she want Papa Bois out of the way?"

Glo's expression darkened, though her voice stayed even. "Because Papa Bois is de balance. And some people, child… dey tink balance is a chain keeping dem back. To reach what dey want, dey feel dey must break it."

Atiba's gut twisted. He shook his head. "None of this matters if I'm stuck here. Can you help me get back? Back to the real world?"

Glo tilted her head, studying him carefully. "Ah could," she admitted. Then she asked, softly but firmly: "But tell me, young one… what yuh intend to do if yuh go back?"

The question hit him like a stone.

For a heartbeat, the answer screamed inside him: go back to Queens. Pretend this never happened. Sell the house, wash his hands of Boisdepin, slip back into the noisy comfort of streets he understood.

His mouth opened… but the words stuck.

He imagined stepping off a plane at JFK, the smell of asphalt and hotdog carts. His friends asking why he came back so soon. His mother smiling smugly when she heard he was selling the house.

And yet…

The memory of the stag at the funeral burned behind his eyes. The children laughing in the streets of Boisdepin. The faces in the old photographs in Wilberforce's house. The ache he'd felt when villagers spoke of his grandfather with reverence — an ache that felt less like pain and more like hunger.

He dragged a hand across his face, ashamed. "Honestly… my first thought was to run. Just go home and forget all this." He gave a sheepish laugh.

Jumbie barked a laugh, sharp and rough. "Anybody with sense would run." Yet his tone lacked venom. If anything, it was weary admiration.

Glo listened with patient silence, then laid her hand on Atiba's shoulder. "De forest call who it will. And yuh answered honest. Dat's all anyone could ask."

She straightened, turning to Jumbie. Her voice shifted — tender, but carrying authority. "Now hear meh. Yuh task is to see dis boy back home. Once it done, consider yuh debt to me repaid."

The air shifted.

Jumbie's face twisted; shock, then resistance. His jaw worked as though grinding words he didn't want to say. "What? Yuh serious?"

"Yes," Glo said softly. "It's time. Time for you to rediscover who yuh are. Yuh doh belong here, Jumbie."

For the first time, he looked smaller. Vulnerable. His gaze flicked to her, then away, as though afraid she'd see too much in his eyes.

"Ah eh want to leave yuh," he muttered, so quiet it was nearly lost under the rush of the river.

Glo's hand brushed his arm, a fleeting caress heavy with meaning. "And ah never want to let yuh go. But yuh been bound too long. Yuh debt is over, boy. Free yourself. Find yourself."

Atiba, watching, suddenly felt like an intruder. The weight of their history pressed into the space, the way Jumbie's gruffness softened when she spoke, the way she looked at him with unguarded affection.

Finally Jumbie gave a stiff nod.

Glo turned back to Atiba, her voice steady once more. "Wilberforce believe in you, child. He leave yuh his bangle. De stag appear to you. Trust dat you worthy. But de path forward? Dat is yours alone."

Atiba swallowed. "And if I see the stag again?"

Her smile was soft, wise, the faintest shadow of sadness behind it. "Be yourself."

The words rang simple but true. "Now go," she said gently.

Reluctantly, Atiba rose. Jumbie followed, posture tense, every line of his body resisting but obeying. Together they stepped toward the edge of the clearing, where the oppressive forest shadows waited like a curtain.

Both paused. Atiba glanced back, taking in Glo's majesty one last time — the way the light seemed to cling to her, bending in reverence. Jumbie looked back too, but his gaze held something else: raw loss, the look of a son leaving his mother forever.

Then they disappeared into the gloom.

Glo stayed where she was, her hands folded in her lap. "Will," she whispered with a fond smile. "Yuh pick a good one."

The clearing grew quiet. Too quiet. Even the river seemed to hush its song.

From the far edge of the light, the shadows thickened. Something stepped forward. The stranger was tall, broad-shouldered, dressed in a perfectly pressed cream suit that gleamed faintly despite the gloom. His shoes were polished black, his tie blood-red, and at his chest pocket sat a folded square of silk, stark white like a funeral flower. His skin was the color of dark teak, smooth as lacquer, and his hair was oiled back into a slick, severe wave.

His grin came first. Wide. Hungry. Too many teeth for one mouth.

Glo's gaze hardened, her coils tightening beneath the water. "Who are you?"

The man gave a slow, exaggerated bow, one arm sweeping out. "Mr. Heartmann," he said in a singsong voice, every syllable of his Bajan drawl sharp as broken glass. "At your service… though not for your sake. I come on behalf of my employer."

He straightened, his grin widening. A faint twitch rattled through his jaw, making one cheek spasm unnaturally before settling back into his wolfish smile.

"You shouldn't be here," Glo said coldly.

"Dis is meh domain."

Her eyes narrowed.

"I suppose yuh here to kill de boy. To snuff out Papa Bois' line."

Heartmann clutched his chest, gasping theatrically as though wounded.

Then he laughed; a dry, high-pitched cackle that echoed too long, like glass cracking in the night. "The boy? Oh, no, no, Mama. Not him. Not ever him."

He leaned forward, and the clearing seemed to tilt toward his presence. "You see, the path here… it had to be opened. A door that required love, grief, desperation." His tongue darted out unnaturally, flicking across his teeth. "It only took a whisper. A push. The right heart in the right place. And she… oh, she delivered beautifully."

Glo's coils stirred the water, her radiant glow brightening. "Yuh dare."

Heartmann's body twitched again, this time his head snapping once to the side like a marionette, a crack of bone echoing in the silence. Then, as if nothing had happened, he looked back at her, smiling wider than before. "Dare?" he repeated, voice syrupy and sick. "My dear Mama D'leau, I've come to collect. My employer wants a prize. And I… I want the sweetest heart I've ever tasted."

He raised his cutlass from the shadows of his coat, the steel shimmering not with light but with a strange, oily black sheen, as though it had been drinking darkness itself.

His body twitched once more, a puppet-like jerk, before his grin returned. "And yours, Mama… is the heart I've been waiting for."

Glo rose, radiant and terrible, coils thrashing, light spilling from her skin like the breaking dawn.

The forest held its breath. The serpent and the madman faced one another, poised for war.

# CHAPTER 12 - ESME

sme stood alone in the empty lot, arms wrapped around herself, the dawn still nothing more than a rumor at the edge of the sky. The shadows at her feet had changed.

Once obedient, once silent, they now rose and fell with a strange breath, rippling like something alive beneath glass. They whispered… not with words, but with pressure. A nudge behind her ribs. A tug at the base of her skull. An ache that hummed with one name.

Levi.

She stared at the trembling dark around her shoes and swallowed hard. The last time she'd been this close to the seam, she had thrown someone else through it.

But Mr. Brown's voice haunted the thin air. He had said "waiting," not "gone." A hair's-breadth difference that had cracked something in her chest.

Esme knelt and set her palms on the asphalt. It was still faintly warm from the lost day.

"Levi," she whispered. "If you hear me… if you feel me…ah coming." The shadows shivered, thrilled.

She stood, wiped her face with the heel of her hand, and closed her eyes. She gathered the threads of shadow she had taught herself to weave—the way a room's light pushed into corners, the way a person's outline stamped itself on the floor. She let those threads spill from her palms, let them pool, let them layer. Her own shadow deepened, rich with a blue-black sheen that turned the lot into a darkened well.

"Open," she breathed.

The air thinned. Asphalt became dusk. Then something beneath the dusk shifted sideways, like the world had pulled a curtain.

The seam blinked.

Esme hesitated.

Her first step felt like treason. Her second, like forgiveness. On the third, the world let go.

As her ankle slid through, the shadows lunged to meet her—warm, slick, eager. They climbed her calves and clung to her thighs like surf and undertow, pulling, pressing, kissing her bones with cold. She forced herself not to fight it, to breathe the way Tanty had taught her in childhood—slow, long, from the belly. The seam widened. The darkness swallowed her hips, her waist, her chest…

…and shivered, pleased.

She never saw the other shiver it made.

At the edge of her shadow, a ripple lifted, thin as a blade's reflection, and a sliver of night peeled away from the rest. It had weight. It had teeth. It had a grin the color of bruised moonlight. It flowed where her shadow flowed, lay flat where her shadow lay flat, and when she stepped fully into the seam, it slid with her… so close its breath was her breath, so near its weight became her weight.

Esme did not feel it. The seam closed, and the parking lot was empty. For Atiba, the shadows must have been quicksand: suffocating, crushing, hostile, like it was for anyone else unfortunate enough to be thrown in. But for Esme, the seam opened like a sky. The darkness wasn't heavy; it was infinite. She floated, not sinking, but suspended as though a great cosmic tide had caught her. Her hair drifted around her face, her arms outstretched, her body buoyed by unseen currents.

The black wasn't black at all. It was threaded with constellations—faint starlight twinkling and bending, pulsing to the rhythm of her own heart. The void welcomed her. It didn't shove her out as it might have had anyone but her. It knew her, the way a body knew its blood.

She drifted, limbs light, her breath easy. She didn't choke. She didn't panic. She exhaled, and the void exhaled back, as if the place itself was breathing with her. For a moment, she felt whole, an extension of this realm, not an intruder.

"Levi," she whispered. The name rippled across the star-threads, and they pulsed faintly in answer.

For the briefest second, she thought she saw him—a boy's silhouette in the constellation-light, head tilted, eyes soft. But then the tide shifted, and the vision slipped away like smoke.

The stars bent, coalescing into a line. She knew without thinking: this was her path. She reached, and the seam answered. The world folded forward, and she stepped through.

Color died here. Every green was indigo, every brown was iron. The sky had no clouds, only the slow churn of a purple-black sea turned on its head. The air smelled of wet earth and the tin-snap tang of lightning long after a storm. Sound moved strangely: the drag of her own breath came back to her a half heartbeat late, like an echo walking behind.

Esme stood very still, calves dripping with shadow like oil. She concentrated, testing the shape of her power.

In the living world, her shadows bent quick as thought. Here… they argued. They didn't refuse her—they negotiated. She could coax them into a blade, and the blade would be a river that wanted to be a road. She could command a veil, and the veil would be fog with bad manners. Every request came with a price: more focus, more will, more memory.

She swallowed. "Fine," she whispered. "We go play by yuh rules."

Somewhere to her left, a moan unspooled, a sound thick as honey gone sour. She turned and saw the headstones first, scattered like crooked teeth across a hill that wasn't the Boisdepin cemetery and yet felt like it had been peeled from its skin. The plots gaped. The dirt heaved. And above the sinking ground, wraiths floated—bodies torn from their borders, flickering between smoke and matter. Their mouths hung open in silent wails. Their eyes burned with a pale, starved light.

Esme exhaled through her nose. "I eh here for you."

The shadow at her back swelled like a pleased cat. She didn't feel the other shadow swell with it.

She wrapped herself in a thin skin of night, just enough to blur, just enough to dim, and moved along the treeline.

The jumbies tilted toward her, drawn, tasting. The heat they gave off made the air throb. Two drifted close; she raised a hand and whispered a shape.

The shadow in her palm flattened, then folded, then rose into a narrow pane that hummed like a tuning fork. The first wraith touched it and recoiled, the second slid along its edge like water down a blade.

Not a wall, but a river that remembered being straight. "Good enough," Esme murmured, and kept moving.

She pressed forward, following memory and instinct. Levi. She repeated his name until it became a metronome. The forest warped, branches bent wrong, leaves that seemed to breathe, roots that sighed when she stepped on them. Eventually, the taste of the air changed—cleaner, greener, undercut with lime and bark. She slowed, chest tight.

The river's song rose ahead of her, patient, endless, unmistakable. And the shadows around her feet trembled with something that was not warning, not defiance. Expectation.

Esme squared her shoulders. "Levi… ah comin'."

And she stepped deeper into the Jumbie World, never noticing the second shadow that trailed her, smiling, silent, and hungry.

A shape darted along the canopy, a child in a straw hat, feet turned the wrong way. The Douen watched her without eyes. One giggled, and wind moved through the branches like fingers through beads. Esme looked away. "Not today."

Something inside her shadow stirred, pleased by the sight of small, lost things.

She stopped at a sink of ground where roots formed a low cave. The earth here felt quiet. Tucked. Good enough to breathe.

Esme slid under, sat with her knees to her chest, and pressed her back against the cool tangle. She closed her eyes and forced her thoughts to slow. The Jumbie World didn't want panic; it wanted posture. She pictured Levi again. She pictured the last thing she'd said to him. (It had been a lie. "I'll fix it." It had also been the only truth she had left.) She smoothed that memory flat and used it as a map.

"Show me where he clingin'," she whispered to the dark. "Show me where he stick."

For a long moment, nothing. Then the earth sighed beneath her, and a line of cold traced from her heel to her hip to her spine, as if the world had drawn a path up her bones and lit it with frost.

Esme opened her eyes. "Good. Thank you."

She crawled out from under the roots and stood…

…and felt lighter.

Not freer. Not safer. Simply… missing something. Like a weight that had been riding her shoulders had slid away in the night.

She frowned and glanced down. Her shadow lay under her in the purple light, steady as her pulse. It touched the dirt, touched her heels, touched the trees. Whole. Still, the sense of absence clung to her like a scent she couldn't place.

"Move," she told herself. "Move before yuh think too much."

She followed the cold the earth had drawn in her. North, or what passed for it here. The sky didn't change, but the taste of the air did. More metal, less moss. Once she heard laughter, that high, bent sound that children made when they were about to be wicked. Once she heard a long, low howl that pulled something grief-struck out of the center of her chest. She swallowed it back down and walked faster.

Time buckled. Minutes became a mile; an hour fit in the space between two breaths. She kept repeating his name, and the world kept answering with a path of cold up her bones. Finally, the trees thinned to a web of black lace and the ground pitched downward. In the hollow below, the air was hot, too hot, and the darkness swam in a tight, mean circle.

"Levi?" Her voice came out small. The heat pressed against her eyelids like hands. "Levi, you here?"

And then she saw him. Or what was left.

Levi's body lay curled in the roots at the center of the snag, cradled like some terrible offering. His flesh had shrunken to leather, pulled taut against brittle bone. Patches of skin clung in darkened sheets, cracked and peeling, while in other places it had sunk entirely, leaving hollows that showed the sharp ridges of ribs and spine. His hair, once thick and unruly, hung in sparse, brittle strands across the dirt, tangled with roots and rot. His mouth gaped half-open, lips long withered away to expose teeth the color of old ivory.

There was no breath. No movement. No spark. Only the stillness of a body long surrendered to time.

The sight of his sunken sockets, the empty caverns where eyes had collapsed, sent Esme's stomach pitching. She had told herself she was ready for this, that she had buried him once already, in shadow, that she had steeled her heart for whatever waited here. But the truth struck her harder than any curse: Levi was gone. Entirely gone.

Her knees buckled. She hit the dirt with a sob that ripped out of her like something broken loose inside her chest. The sound echoed in the hollow, jagged and raw. "Oh God… Levi…"

She crawled closer on shaking hands, reaching but stopping short, as though touching him would make the finality real. The smell of dry rot and earth hung heavy, coating her throat. Her hand hovered above his ribcage, inches from the brittle curve of bone beneath skin like parchment.

Seven years. Seven years since she had driven the knife through him. Seven years since his scream split the sky and the Day of Darkness swallowed everything. She had pictured him a thousand ways in her guilt, but nothing prepared her for this. Not the hollow shell. Not the silence.

Esme pressed her palms into the dirt, bowing her head until her forehead nearly touched the ground. A keening breath tore from her, ragged and shaking. "I did this," she whispered, voice breaking. "I did this to you."

The snag creaked in the wind, roots tightening around the corpse as though the forest itself had been keeping vigil all these years. Levi had not been preserved by magic, not suspended in some secret sleep. He had rotted as any man would, left to time and memory.

And that, more than anything, broke her.

Her fingers clawed into the soil. Tears burned down her face.

Duped. She had been duped by Mr. Brown. She had killed Atiba, enraged Prak, and laid the path for whatever plan Mr. Brown was weaving— all for nothing.

Her sobs shook the hollow. Finally, with a shudder, she turned away, forcing the image of Levi's ruined body from view. She stumbled away, aimless, hollow. She wandered, barely noticing the wraiths that stirred in the trees, their pale eyes fixed on her.

Esme stumbled through the Jumbie World like a ghost. Her steps dragged; her breath came shallow. Every root snagged her ankles, every branch cut at her arms, but she didn't raise her hands.

The memory of Levi's withered face clung to her. His eyes, empty, but not gone. His chest, struggling against death like a candle guttering in a storm.

She had failed him. She had failed Prak. She had failed herself.

Mr. Brown's words gnawed in the marrow of her bones: "Waiting, not gone."

What lay before her eyes screamed otherwise. Levi's body was a husk, skin clinging to bone, lips shriveled from teeth, the shell of someone she had loved. It should have been the end.

But she would not accept it. No. Brown had not lied. This was only the body, just the vessel. Levi was stronger than this. Somewhere beyond the veil, her brother was still there. Waiting, like Brown said. Waiting for her.

Her throat tightened, hot tears cutting down her cheeks. If she believed he was gone, then she had damned him twice: first with her hand, then with her grief. She would not. She could not.

He was waiting. Not gone. He had to be.

She whispered it to herself until the words felt less like hope and more like truth.

Her legs gave out. She sank to her knees in the black soil, her fingers curling weakly into the dirt. For the first time since she was a child, she prayed. Not to God. He had long since abandoned her family. Not to Tanty, either; Tanty had cursed them. She prayed to nothing. Just sound spilling from her mouth.

The forest didn't answer. Instead, it sent jumbies.

The moans came low at first, like a sigh of rotting wood. Then louder, hungrier, echoing from every angle. Shadows thickened, pulling themselves free of the crooked trees. Wraith-bodies swam into being, their mouths stretched into silent howls, their pale eyes fever-bright.

Esme didn't move. She tipped her head back against the tree behind her and closed her eyes. Her shoulders slumped. Her lips parted in a whisper: "Fine. Take meh, then."

The wraiths circled closer, their smoke-bodies writhing, their heat making the air throb. One drifted low, reaching with claws made of half-shadow, half-bone. Esme didn't flinch. She almost welcomed the touch.

But then... A shout ripped through the clearing. "HEY!"

The jumbies snapped toward the voice. Esme's eyes shot open. Atiba.

He stumbled into view, chest heaving, eyes wild. He looked like he didn't even understand why he was there, why his body had carried him forward. His arms were raised, shielding Esme with his own frame, though his voice trembled when he barked: "Stay the hell away from her!"

The nearest wraith recoiled, as if confused by the audacity.

Esme blinked at him in disbelief, her lips trembling. Alive. He was alive. And not just alive. Standing between her and death.

Something cracked inside her chest. The emptiness that had swallowed her began to leak light, just a sliver. If Atiba still breathed, then maybe not all her choices had been in vain. Maybe redemption wasn't a lie.

"Atiba…" she whispered, her voice breaking.

He shot her a sharp look, eyes narrow, posture stiff. "Don't get it twisted. I don't even know why I did that." His jaw clenched. "It just… happened."

Still, the heat in his words didn't hide the truth: he had chosen, instinctively, to protect her.

# CHAPTER 13 - PRAK

The old woman's hut waited in the shadows like it had been expecting him.

Prak stopped at the edge of the clearing, his chest heaving. For a moment he almost turned back. He didn't like asking for help, never had. And this woman… she knew too much. Saw too much. Every instinct in him told him to bare his teeth, to growl until she gave him what he wanted.

But Wilberforce's voice rose in his memory, steady as stone: Respect does more than strength ever could, Prakesh. So Prak swallowed his snarl.

Forced his claws to stay sheathed. And stepped forward.

The old woman sat outside, as though she had been waiting, cross-legged by her fire, eyes half-closed, the smoke curling through her hair like a crown. The usual eerie whispers and chittering of the Douen that called this clearing home were absent. Strange, but not worth following up on with so much currently at stake. When Prak approached, her lids lifted, and she tilted her head as though listening to something far away.

"What it is have yuh so kilkité, boy?" she asked.

"Trouble," he replied. "Big trouble."

"Ah feel it," she murmured. "A tearin. A stirring dat doh belong in this world. Someting happen, chile. Someting bad."

Prak dropped into a crouch across from her fire, his cutlass balanced across his knees. His voice was hoarse, scraped raw from the howl still clinging to his throat.

"Ah feel him," he said. "Atiba. He alive. But not here. Not in Boisdepin. It was like his fear rush through me, like it was mine."

The old woman's eyes sharpened. "Tell me what yuh see."

Prak's claws flexed against the blade's handle. He forced the words out. "She was dere. At de graveyard. Esme. She say she trade Atiba for Levi. Den she shadow…" His jaw clenched, fury trembling through him. "She shadow spread across the whole cemetery. And when it clear… she was gone. And so was he."

The old woman inhaled slowly, her gaze flickering with memory. "Levi," she whispered. "De boy who uses to carry shadow like a curse. A remnant of he family's binding. Ah know he power. Ah remember it. But you…" she leaned forward, her voice sharp, suspicious. "How dis Esme could wield de same?"

Prak's throat tightened. His chest rose and fell in heavy, uneven bursts. "Dat… da'is a long story," he ground out. "Longer dan we have right now. But jus' know," His voice cracked on the words. "Esme take it from Levi. When she… when she kill him."

For a moment, the only sound was the fire snapping. The old woman's expression softened, but her eyes stayed hard.

"So," she said slowly, "de shadow is she own now. And wit' it, she send de boy where no one belong."

She drew a long breath and let it out through her nose. "Into de Jumbie World."

Prak's head jerked up, his eyes flashing. "De Jumbie World? Dat eh make sense. Even with de veil torn, tings does leak out, yes—but dey doh pass through from dis side. Doh cross over like dat."

The old woman gave a low chuckle, dry as leaves in drought. "You only tink you know, boy. Yuh understanding shallow, like water in a gutter. Yuh see pieces, not de whole."

Prak's teeth bared in a snarl. "And what, yuh know better?"

Her eyes glittered through the smoke. "I know enough. You ever been inside Levi's shadow world? You must have. Everybody close to him did, whether dey want to or not."

Prak's claws tightened on the cutlass. He remembered the suffocating dark, the way it clung to him, pulled him under. He gave a short, tense nod.

"Dat place," she said, pointing a knotted finger toward him, "was not de Jumbie World. It was only a passageway. A seam Levi hold open with his curse. A place in-between, halfway house for de dead an' de living. If he had pushed further, if he had reached past de edges of dat shadow… he coulda step through. He coulda reach de other side."

Prak frowned, his ears twitching with unease. "So yuh sayin'… all dis time, Levi coulda cross into de Jumbie World?"

The old woman's gaze deepened, her face solemn. "Yes. But he never know, or never dare. He gift wasn't only a curse, chile. It was a key."

Prak swallowed, his jaw tight. His voice cracked when he spoke again. "So how Esme… how she manage it?"

"Because she hold de shadow now," the woman said flatly. "And with de veil already torn, de door doh resist her. She open it, whether she know what she was doin' or not. And she send Atiba through."

The fire popped, sparks snapping between them. Prak's chest heaved, his breath ragged.

The woman leaned closer, her voice dropping into something almost reverent. "Understand me, Prak. The Jumbie World not just some dark place. It is half of creation itself. Once, long before memory, it was not separate. Jumbies walk as free as agouti or wild fowl. Dey laugh with man, dey eat with man. De world was whole. But some force, man, god, or monster, split it apart. Nobody know for sure who, or why. Only dat from dat tearing came two halves: de flesh-and-blood world, and de Jumbie World. Mirror to mirror. Shadow to light."

Her eyes narrowed, her voice edged with warning. "Papa Bois came after de split. Guardian, mediator, protector. His spirit was born out of need. To keep de halves from crushing each other… or swallowing each other whole."

Prak sat frozen, the truth pressing on him like a mountain. The firelight caught his eyes, gleaming with anger and despair.

The old woman's voice softened, but it did not lose its weight. "Now de veil weak. De halves lean toward each other again. Jumbies slip through cracks. And now? Atiba walk on de other side."

Prak dragged a hand over his face, every muscle trembling. "And if he cyah find a way back…?"

The old woman did not answer right away. The silence was louder than any words. Finally, she spoke. "Den yuh cousin will be trapped there. Until he nothin' but a story."

Prak's knuckles went white on the cutlass' grip. His voice came out low, hoarse. "So what ah supposed to do? Just sit here and wait for Atiba to turn into a story?"

The old woman's eyes narrowed through the rising smoke. "Yuh quick to bare yuh teeth, boy, but not quick to use yuh head. If de boy in de Jumbie World, den de only way to reach him… is to cross."

Prak's pulse kicked. He leaned forward, jaw tight. "Show me how."

For a moment she only stared, the firelight catching in her eyes. Prak's mind raced ahead of her silence, filling in the things she might demand: a life for a life, blood on the earth, some sacred debt that would bind him tighter than chains. The kind of bargain men didn't walk away from whole. He braced for it, shoulders coiled, already readying himself to pay.

But then she arched a brow, her lips curling into something that was neither smile nor sneer. "I go do it free. Just this once."

Relief punched through him so sharp it almost hurt. He swallowed hard, words rougher than he meant. "Thank yuh."

The old woman began to lay things out around the fire: bundles of dried herbs, bowls of river water, bones carved with strange sigils. She hummed under her breath, low, resonant, like a lullaby buried under centuries of dust.

"The veil doh open easy for you," she said, scattering the herbs into the flames. Sparks hissed green. "Yuh not de heir. De forest eh choose you. But dere is a way. De stag will come."

Prak stiffened, his breath catching. "De stag?"

She nodded slowly. "De essence of Papa Bois. De same creature dat test every heir. It will decide if yuh cross. Not me."

Prak's chest tightened. He had heard the stories, of course, Wilberforce had told him late at night, voice hushed, eyes sharp. But he had never seen it. Never thought he would.

The woman's voice dropped into a hush. "If yuh touch it, Prak, de power of Papa Bois could be yours. But yuh heart must be clean. If yuh reach for it wid envy or hunger, it will tear yuh apart."

Her words twisted in his gut. For as long as he could remember, he had wanted that mantle. Had dreamed of it. To stand where Wilberforce had stood. To be more than just his shadow. And now it was close. Close enough to taste.

The fire flared higher, fed by herbs and bone. Its smoke bent unnaturally, curling against the wind, forming strange spirals that didn't dissipate. The shadows around the clearing thickened, stretching too long, as though reaching toward the blaze.

Prak's skin prickled. Something was happening.

The old woman's chanting deepened, her voice pulling low, scraping the marrow of the earth itself. She cast another handful of herbs into the fire, and the flames shifted from orange to a molten green, licking upward like the tongues of unseen beasts.

Then the air tore. Not with sound, but with weight.

The clearing pressed inward, like reality itself had bent a knee. The shadows at the edge of the fire convulsed, trembling as if caught between two breaths. They deepened, then thinned, then deepened again, pulsing like a heartbeat.

Prak staggered back, clutching his chest. He couldn't see a door. Couldn't see a curtain. But he felt it. A threshold, raw and wrong, humming in the roots beneath his feet and the air in his lungs. The veil wasn't just here—it was reacting.

"The veil doh show itself to mortal eyes," the old woman said, her face lit with green firelight. "But when it close to breaking, yuh can feel it, taste it, hear it in de blood. Right dere." She nodded toward a patch of shadow that had stretched impossibly tall against the far tree, its edges rippling like liquid.

Prak's pulse hammered. The shadow swayed though no wind touched it. Every instinct screamed at him to look away, but he couldn't. The thing was waiting.

The stag stepped through.

Its body burned with quiet light, its antlers vast enough to scrape the sky, though it never disturbed a branch. The fire bent toward it. The unnatural shadow bent away from it. Its hooves left no prints, but every step pressed into Prak's ribs like a drumbeat.

He fell to his knees, his hand lifting, shaking, yearning to brush its muzzle. His grandfather's mantle. His dream. His birthright. For a heartbeat, joy surged hot through him, flooding his chest until he nearly buckled. Maybe Wilberforce had been wrong. Maybe the forest had chosen him after all. The thought filled him with a fierce, almost childlike relief, a warmth that burned away the grief and rage if only for a moment. His eyes stung. His lips even parted, ready to laugh, ready to thank the stag for proving what he had always believed deep down…

But then it stilled. Its massive head tilted, the great crown of antlers catching the firelight. Its eyes did not shine with welcome. They weighed him. Measured him. The warmth drained from his chest, replaced by a hollow pressure, as though the forest itself pressed down on his ribs. This wasn't a gift. It wasn't a correction. It was a question.

Would he take what was never meant for him? Would he reach, and claim, and usurp?

The stag's muzzle hovered close, close enough to touch. Close enough to seize everything he thought he wanted.

Prak's breath trembled. Every memory of failure, of being overlooked, of standing in Wilberforce's shadow rose up to claw at him. He had trained harder, fought longer, bled more than anyone. He had carried the weight of the village when no one else would. And still the stag had gone to Atiba. A boy who knew nothing of this land. Nothing of the fight. Nothing of the blood Wilberforce shed to keep the balance.

It would be so easy. One touch. One choice. The forest would bend. The title would be his. And no one, no cousin, no foreign heir, no shade of Wilberforce's disapproval, could take it away.

His hand hovered, inches from the stag's muzzle. His pulse thundered. His claws flexed, aching to close the gap. But in the hollow of that temptation, another thought surfaced.

Atiba carried Wilberforce's bangle. Still looked at Prak with trust. If Prak took this now, what would he become? Not a guardian. Not a protector.

A thief.

His hand shook violently. His chest ached with longing. And then, with a half-snarl, half-sob, he forced his arm back to his side.

The stag's eyes burned brighter, not with anger, but acknowledgment. It stamped once, the ground quaking under its hooves. Then, slowly, it turned, antlers brushing the air like branches swaying in a storm.

And just like that, it vanished, dissolving into smoke and firelight until only the shadows of the clearing remained. Prak stayed kneeling, his hand still trembling at his side, his breath ragged. The warmth that had surged through him was gone now, replaced with something heavier, an emptiness that ached like loss.

The old woman's voice broke the silence. "Yuh pass," she said simply.

Prak's head snapped up, his eyes narrowing. "Pass?" His voice cracked with disbelief. "Ah refuse. Ah turn away. How dat is passing?"

The old woman leaned on her staff, her face unreadable in the firelight. "Because yuh could'a take it. Yuh wanted to take it. Every drop of yuh blood scream for it. But yuh didn't. Dat is de test."

Her eyes softened, though her tone stayed firm. "Papa Bois doh just protect de forest, boy. He protect de balance. Power without restraint is only hunger. Yuh show restraint. Yuh show respect. Dat is worth more dan claws or teet'."

Prak looked away, his jaw tight. Shame prickled under his skin, but beneath it, a something stirred—something like dignity.

The woman moved closer, her shadow stretching long across the dirt. "De stag wasn't here to choose yuh. It was here to weigh yuh. To see if yuh heart was twisted with envy. If yuh did touch it, Atiba woulda lose he path. Yuh woulda claim a crown dat was never meant for you…and de forest woulda rot with de theft."

Prak's throat clenched. "So ah really was never meant…" He stopped himself, swallowing hard.

The old woman's gaze softened further, almost pitying. "Maybe not de crown. But de forest still need yuh. Yuh cousin still need yuh. What yuh do here prove yuh is more dan a shadow standing in Wilberforce place. You is your own man. And yuh about to walk where few ever return from."

Her staff pressed into the dirt, and the fire behind her roared higher, flaring green. A seam of shadow stretched out from the flames, bending toward the treeline, quivering like a curtain caught in a breeze that only Prak could feel.

"De way open," she said. "Go find him."

Prak stared at the quivering shadow. His body felt heavy, his heart heavier. But under it all, a steel resolve burned through the doubt. He rose to his feet, cutlass in hand.

"For 'Tiba," he muttered. And he stepped into the dark.

# CHAPTER 14 - ESME

Esme had braced for the claws. For the teeth. For the end she had half-convinced herself she deserved.

But then with Atiba's sudden appearance, something inside her twisted.

For the first time since stepping into this cursed world, Esme wanted to live… not for herself, but because this boy threw himself between her and the shadows with nothing but trembling hands and stubborn impulse.

And then the shadows erupted like a storm.

A jagged fissure tore across the clearing, black lightning without light, splitting the gloom apart. The air buckled as if struck by thunder, trees bowing in submission, leaves spiraling upward in a cyclone of ash and grit.

Something moved inside that eruption. Someone.

He came like a thrown blade, headlong and merciless. His body hit the first wraith with such force that its shape folded inward, shrieking like metal being bent past its breaking point. Shadows whipped from his arms and shoulders, writhing serpents of black flame that coiled, lashed, devoured.

Another wraith lunged—he caught it by the throat mid-charge, its smoky body thrashing against him, and slammed it to the ground so hard the earth split open. The impact made the rest hesitate. Just for a heartbeat. But that was all he needed.

With a roar, the man hurled himself deeper into the swarm. Claws of shadow tore from his hands, carving through their flickering bodies, shredding them into nothing. Every strike was violent rhythm—too practiced, too precise, too much like him.

Esme's breath left her in a single, ragged gasp.

This wasn't Levi. It couldn't be. She had just seen his corpse, withered and still in the seam. She had mourned him, damned herself for losing him. And yet... this stranger didn't just look like her brother, he fought like him too. The same wild cadence. The same crooked grin hidden in his fury. The same shadows that bent too eagerly, as though they had waited for him. Her mind told her it was impossible. Her heart whispered it might still be him.

Her lips trembled, and the name slipped out before she could stop it. "Levi...?"

The storm swallowed her whisper. He didn't hear. He didn't turn. He only fought harder, as if the chaos itself was feeding him, and he was glad to be fed.

Esme couldn't take her eyes off him. The way the shadows obeyed, the way his movements blurred between flesh and smoke—it was Levi, and yet it wasn't. She had seen Levi's corpse. She had touched his still, withered skin. This man could not be him.

And yet... her chest ached with recognition. She almost missed the boy beside her.

Atiba stood stiff as a branch in a storm, his whole body trembling. His hands twitched, opening and closing uselessly at his sides. His eyes... those wide, terrified eyes... were locked on the stranger tearing the wraiths apart, and Esme saw it clear as day: awe battling terror, a desperate wish that this man was salvation warring with the gut-deep knowledge that he was something far more dangerous.

The shadows burst and hissed around them, and still Atiba didn't move. He looked trapped between fight and flight, his legs refusing either. Esme's own breath hitched as she watched him, young, untested, still vibrating with fear, and something sharp twisted in her chest.

She had sent him to die. She had looked him in the eye and let the ground swallow him, convincing herself it was worth it; Levi's life for Atiba's. She had told herself the boy was just collateral, a necessary sacrifice. And yet here he was. Not dead. Not broken. But standing in front of her, trembling with fear, still putting his body between her and the dark as if some part of him believed she was worth protecting.

The shame of it burned hotter than the wraiths' suffocating heat. She wanted to tell him to move, to run, to save himself—but the words stuck like thorns in her throat. Maybe because some part of her didn't want him to. Some part of her needed to believe she could still be worth saving.

The last wraith shrieked, its starved body writhing as it surged toward them, its claws glowing with a pale, desperate hunger. Atiba flinched, shoulders tight, but his feet still held the line between Esme and the creature.

Esme's breath caught, ready to throw herself forward…

…but she didn't have to.

The stranger was already there.

He hurled himself into the wraith like a man possessed, shadows coiling around his fists like barbed chains. The air cracked with the force of his blow as he drove the wraith down, pinning it against the earth. Its scream split the trees, wild and piercing, before he ripped through its chest with a savage twist. Light burst like shattering glass.

Then silence.

The body dissolved into ash. The smell of cold iron and smoke hung in the air.

The man stood over the ruin, chest heaving, the shadows around him curling back into the earth like they obeyed only him.

The battlefield stank of burnt air and cold earth. Wisps of fading shadow drifted up like smoke after a fire. The man, her brother's doppelganger, stood at the center of it all, his shoulders heaving, his skin slick with sweat and darkness both. His mouth curled faintly—not triumph, not relief, but something darker. A grim satisfaction, as though he fed on the violence.

The stranger straightened, his shoulders rising and falling with the rhythm of battle still burning in his chest. The shadows coiled back into the soil, docile again, leaving only a man where a monster had been.

Esme's breath snagged. The set of his jaw. The slope of his nose. The cut of his cheekbones. The steady, dangerous stillness after the storm of violence.

Levi.

Her heart lurched, violent and painful, like it had slammed into her ribs. It was him. It had to be. He looked exactly like her brother, only older, harder. As though this was who Levi might have become if he had lived those missing years, every line in his body sharpened by struggle, by survival.

Exactly like the young man she had loved, mourned, damned herself to save.

"No…" she whispered, stumbling forward, her throat raw. "Levi…"

A blinding flash of light split the trees. A scream followed, high and piercing, so full of agony that it rooted Esme to the spot.

Atiba snapped rigid, eyes wide. The stranger, Levi, whipped toward the sound like a hound catching a scent. Neither hesitated. Both bolted, the youth and the man, sprinting toward the scream as if they knew the voice that made it.

Esme's pulse hammered. She didn't think. She just followed, tearing through the warped forest after them. Branches whipped at her face. The ground seemed to pitch and curl under her feet, trying to throw her off course, but she kept running.

The trees broke into a clearing.

And there, bathed in the purple haze of the Jumbie World's false light, stood a nightmare.

Heartmann.

His shirt clung to his body, crimson and wet, blood dripping from his chin, his arms, his hair. In one hand he clutched a cutlass, its blade blackened, smoking as though it had been pulled straight from a forge. In the other, a heart beat. A real, wet, still-beating heart, twitching against his palm like a bird caught in a fist.

Behind him lay a corpse. Esme's stomach hollowed.

The woman's face was slack, her dark eyes glazed in death, her mouth slightly open as though caught mid-breath. But her body… it wasn't human. From the waist up, yes—skin still faintly glowing, features haunting even in stillness. But below, a massive serpent's tail sprawled across the clearing, its iridescent scales slashed and streaked with blood. The coils lay hacked and ruined, once a symbol of power now desecrated in the dirt.

Esme clutched her chest, bile clawing its way up her throat. She had never seen Millie's body… only the news reports, only the cold, sterile words of strangers telling her that her best friend was gone. But staring at this slack face, this brutalized corpse, her imagination betrayed her. This was what Millie might have looked like. Alone. Defiled. The warmth stripped from her, left for the world to gawk at. Esme gagged, pressing her knuckles to her lips, grief and guilt tangling until she could barely breathe.

Levi… the man who looked like Levi… stood rigid as stone. His fists clenched so tight his knuckles whitened, shadows writhing around his arms as though ready to burst. His chest heaved with silent fury, the cords of his neck tight. His jaw trembled with the barely restrained need to rip Heartmann apart.

Atiba's reaction was the opposite. His whole body recoiled, his shoulders jerking back like a child who had just seen a nightmare made flesh. His wide eyes locked on the serpent's coils, and his lips parted as though he might scream but no sound came. His knees bent as though ready to buckle.

He looked like a boy trying to make himself small in a tempest far too big for him.

The contrast hit Esme like a hammer. Rage in one, horror in the other and herself caught somewhere between, drowning in guilt.

Heartmann's head snapped toward her, his grin spreading wide across his blood-smeared face. His eyes lit with manic delight, and the corner of his mouth twitched, like laughter bubbling up from somewhere too deep.

"Well, look who come," he drawled in a sing-song Bajan accent, almost playful.

In his fist, the heart twitched. It wasn't just meat. It was alive, still beating, still pumping, still steaming in the cold air. Each pulse sent thick rivulets of blood snaking down his wrist, spattering the ground in slow, heavy drops.

Heartmann squeezed, and the muscle convulsed, a grotesque parody of life. "Perfect timing, sweetheart."

He lifted the heart to his lips and kissed it, smearing his mouth red. "Thank you." His voice turned honey-sweet, mocking.

"Couldn't have done it without yuh. Yuh shadow trick? That lil' doorway you carve to slip in here? That was the only way I could step foot in dis place. You open it, and I slip right in behind yuh. Quiet. Easy. And yuh never even notice."

Esme staggered back, her breath ragged, horror knotting her insides as Heartmann's grin split into something feral, something inhuman.

"Played like a fiddle," he cooed. "And now, look, door wide open, prize in my hand. All thanks to you."

And in that moment she knew: she hadn't just damned Atiba, she had opened the door for this monster to butcher something sacred.

# CHAPTER 15 - ATIBA

The clearing stank of iron and smoke. The air was so heavy with blood that every breath scraped Atiba's throat raw.

Glo's killer stood in the center like a man born to it, shirt clinging wet to his skin, cutlass blackened and dripping, the heart in his hand twitching in grotesque rhythm. Behind him, her coils lay ruined across the dirt, gleaming scales dulling as her lifeblood soaked into the soil. Her slack face turned toward the sky, glassy eyes catching the false purple light.

Atiba's stomach lurched. He wanted to scream, to vomit, to run—anything but stand here. He clutched his sides, trembling so hard his teeth clicked.

He'd thought the Jumbie World couldn't get worse than the wraiths. He'd been wrong.

Beside him, the stranger, the man who called himself a Jumbie, stood stone still. The fury in his body radiated like heat, so strong that even Esme took an unconscious step back.

She looked broken. Her body shook, her hands pressed to her mouth, her eyes wide and glassy. She swayed like the sight alone might knock her over. Atiba swallowed hard. For all her power, for all the terror she'd put him through, right now she looked… small. Like the sheer brutality of the scene had cracked something deep inside her.

His body moved before his mind did, he stepped forward, putting himself between Esme and the monster in the clearing. His fists clenched, useless, but clenched all the same. He didn't even know why. Instinct. Impulse.

The blood-soaked man noticed. His gaze shifted lazily to Atiba, then to the stranger, then back again. His grin sharpened. "Ohhh… look at dis little gathering. The heir. The shade. And the traitor." His tongue darted unnaturally across his teeth, too fast, too slick. "Ain't dis a sweet reunion?"

Atiba's chest heaved. His breath came in sharp, uneven pulls. He felt Esme's hand brush his shoulder, hesitant, trembling. He wanted to shrug her off, to snarl at her to keep her distance. But he didn't. Not this time. His eyes locked on the man's cutlass, still smoking black.

Jumbie finally moved. One step forward. His shoulders squared. His eyes burned into the other man, and his voice came low, rough, dangerous: "Yuh touch she heart. Now ah go tear out yours." The shadows around him surged.

The man's grin spasmed wider, his lips twitching like strings pulled by an unseen hand. "Yes. Yessss. Fight me, shadow-boy. Show me if yuh anyting more than a shell wearin' a dead man's face. Men been callin' me long before dis land even had a name. When a chest give out, when a heart falter sweet in it rhythm, I was de shadow waitin'. Dey call me to follow de last breath, and I always collect. Dey call me Heartmann!" His voice dropped, jagged with hunger. "So tell me, boy, wha' yuh tink go happen when I come for yuh?"

Heartmann. The word rolled through Atiba like a bell toll, deep and final. Not just a name, but something older, darker.

The air trembled. The ground shivered underfoot. For a heartbeat, nothing moved, the tension strung tighter than a bowstring. Then Jumbie stepped forward, shadows flaring like a tornado ripping through a canefield. The earth split with the weight of it. That was his answer.

The air cracked as the two figures collided.

Jumbie moved first, shadows bursting from his frame like wings of ink. He launched across the clearing, fists striking with the weight of thunder. His first blow caught Heartmann square in the chest and sent him skidding backward, boots carving trenches in the blood-soaked dirt. The ground shuddered from the impact.

But Heartmann didn't fall. He straightened, laughing… actually laughing… his ribs visibly dented before snapping back with a sickening pop. "Good," he hissed. "Hit me again."

Jumbie obliged. He spun, his heel slamming into Heartmann's jaw with a crack loud enough to rattle Atiba's teeth. The man's head snapped sideways, but he grinned through the blow, blood streaming from the corner of his mouth. His cutlass whipped upward, carving through the shadows coiled around Jumbie's arms. The steel drank the darkness, sizzling as though feeding on it.

Atiba's breath stuck in his throat. This wasn't a fight—this was something else. Two forces, neither truly human, colliding like storm against storm.

Jumbie roared, his voice carrying like a beast's. Shadows writhed up his fists, lengthening into claws that slashed across Heartmann's chest. Cloth shredded, blood sprayed. But instead of staggering, Heartmann only shivered, his body twitching in grotesque spasms as though the wounds thrilled him. His grin widened, and he drove his boot into Jumbie's stomach, folding him in half and sending him sprawling.

"Not enough," Heartmann crooned. His tongue flicked unnaturally across his teeth. "Not nearly enough."

Jumbie sprang back up, fury in his eyes. He charged again, faster, harder. His fists blurred, each strike snapping like gunfire. Shadows battered Heartmann from every angle—pummeling, tearing, breaking. The ground beneath them split open under the force. Trees bent inward, leaves spiraling in a cyclone of black grit.

Still, Heartmann endured. His body jerked with every blow, bones crunching, flesh tearing. But he didn't stop. He didn't even falter. He absorbed it, withstood it, until finally his cutlass carved a vicious arc, catching Jumbie across the shoulder. The shadow-born warrior staggered, blood spraying. His breathing grew harsher, his movements less precise.

Atiba's chest tightened. He'd never seen anyone fight like this. Jumbie was unstoppable, unstoppable, and still he was faltering.

Heartmann grinned wide enough to split his cheeks. "Tired already?" His voice was still sing-song, still mocking. He seized Jumbie by the throat and lifted him off the ground with terrifying ease, shadows writhing uselessly against his grip.

Esme's breath hitched beside Atiba. He turned, startled, just as her fingers flicked outward. A tendril of shadow, thin and searching, slipped across the ground like spilled ink until it touched Heartmann's own shadow.

The soil beneath him blackened, softening, shifting into a seam that swallowed his weight.

Heartmann staggered, his grin faltering as one leg sank suddenly, knee-deep in darkness that clutched like quicksand. His balance broke, arms jerking wide to steady himself. For the first time, a snarl tore from his lips.

"Move!" Esme's voice cracked through the air, sharp as glass.

Jumbie didn't hesitate. His own shadows surged up around him, coiling like serpents as he launched forward, both fists slamming into Heartmann's chest. The blow erupted with raw force, tearing him free of the seam and sending the madman sprawling hard into the dirt.

The ground shook with the impact.

Atiba stood frozen in awe, his heart hammering. First Jumbie, fighting like a force of nature given flesh. Then Esme, warping the ground itself into shadows that swallowed and clutched like living hands. Monsters. Both of them. And yet, right now, they were the only reason he was still alive.

Heartmann's laugh broke the silence again, ragged but still rising. He pushed himself up slowly, cracks running across his skin like stone under strain. His cutlass gleamed oily black in the half-light.

And Atiba realized this nightmare wasn't anywhere near over.

The clearing was a hurricane of shadows and steel. Jumbie fought hard, every strike precise, his shadows fluid and alive, twisting into claws and whips that seemed to anticipate his intent before he moved. Esme's power tore through beside him, sharp and jagged by comparison, thin tendrils of darkness lashing out like broken glass, cutting across the ground, snapping at

Heartmann's footing. She managed to drag him off balance more than once, shadow seams splitting beneath his boots, but her grip wavered, unsteady. Atiba saw the difference… the way Jumbie commanded his shadows like an extension of his own body, while Esme's flared raw, powerful but rough-edged.

Yet together, even so mismatched, they pressed Heartmann harder than he could have imagined, forcing the madman's grin into something nearer to a smirk.

Heartmann was bleeding, yes. His coat was shredded, his skin cut and bruised. But there was no weakness in him. If anything, he seemed to revel in it, each strike only widening his grin, each wound twitching back into place with a sickening pop.

Atiba could hardly breathe. He stood on the edge of the battle, frozen in awe and terror. He had no powers. Just his two hands and a heart that hammered like it wanted to leap out of his chest.

And then he saw it. Glo's heart.

It lay in the dirt where Heartmann had dropped it during the fray, still slick with blood, still twitching faintly as if refusing to die. Atiba's stomach lurched at the sight, bile burning the back of his throat. The thought of touching it made every instinct scream. But… something else stirred too. A pull. A certainty.

If Heartmann got it back, something terrible would happen. He didn't know how he knew, only that he did. The heart mattered.

He glanced at the battle. Jumbie was slowing, his swings still savage but heavy now, sluggish. Esme peppered Heartmann with razor-thin lances of shadow, tendrils coiling at her heels, but even her ferocity was dimming. Heartmann, meanwhile, only grew sharper, stronger, faster.

Atiba's gut twisted. If he didn't move now, it would be too late.

Swallowing hard, he ducked low and sprinted. Every step felt like stomping through fire, but he forced himself forward, sliding into the blood-slick dirt. His hand closed around the heart. It was warm. Alive. The thrum of it rattled into his bones. He gagged, but didn't let go.

He cast a frantic glance over his shoulder. Heartmann's attention was fixed on Jumbie and Esme, blade and shadows flying. It was his only chance. Atiba scrambled to the base of a crooked tree, clawing at the soil with his bare hands. Dirt caked his nails as he dug, quick and shallow. He dropped the heart into the hollow, covered it with trembling handfuls of earth, and pressed his palms flat until the ground looked undisturbed.

By the time he staggered back to his feet, his hands were shaking, slick with blood and soil both. He forced himself not to look at the spot again, not to give it away.

The moment he stood, the tide turned.

Heartmann slammed Jumbie to the ground, his boot grinding into his chest. Shadows writhed against the pressure, too weak to throw him off. Esme lashed out, a desperate spear of darkness ripping up from the ground and striking Heartmann's shoulder. He barely flinched. With a flick of his cutlass, the shadow split apart like smoke, and then his backhand caught her full in the face. She screamed once before her body hit the ground and went still.

"No!" Atiba shouted before he could stop himself.

Heartmann's head snapped toward him. That grin, stretched and painted in blood, widened. "There you are."

Panic surged. Atiba stumbled backward, his eyes darting to the place he'd buried the heart despite himself. He tried to run, but Heartmann was already on him. A blur of motion, a crushing grip around his throat, and Atiba was lifted off his feet like a child's doll.

"Where is it?" Heartmann crooned, his breath hot with the stink of iron and rot. His cutlass pressed lightly to Atiba's cheek, not cutting, just promising. "Where's Mama D'leau's sweet heart? I can smell it, boy. I can taste it. Don't make me dig through you to find it."

Atiba gagged, his hands clawing at Heartmann's grip. His lungs burned. Still, he shook his head. "I—I don't know what you're talking about."

Heartmann chuckled, low and manic. His grip tightened, spots bursting across Atiba's vision. "Liar. Big man Brown needs it. A ritual. A door that only her heart can open. Do you understand what you're denying me?" He leaned closer, his voice dropping to a conspiratorial whisper. "The end of all this. The beginning of something beautiful."

The cutlass nicked Atiba's cheek, a hot line of pain. "Tell me where it is."

Atiba's body trembled, tears stinging his eyes, but he forced the words out through his choking breath. "Go to hell."

The grin vanished. Heartmann slammed him down into the dirt, boot crushing his chest. Fists rained down, blunt, bone-cracking, relentless. His vision swam, blood filling his mouth.

He couldn't fight back. He couldn't even raise his arms anymore. He was nothing compared to this monster. Nothing like Papa Bois.

How was he supposed to carry his grandfather's mantle? How was he supposed to protect anyone if he couldn't even save himself?

His world dimmed.

And then— A snarl ripped the clearing open.

Heartmann stiffened. Atiba blinked through the haze of pain, and saw a figure bursting from the trees.

Massive. Beast-like. Fur bristling, claws glinting, eyes burning gold. It hit Heartmann like a landslide, ripping him off Atiba with such force the earth itself split.

Atiba coughed, dragging air back into his battered lungs. He blinked up at the monster looming over him—half-man, half-beast, shoulders hunched with power, fangs bared in fury. For a second, he thought it was some new terror come to finish him.

Then it spoke. "Get up, boy."

Atiba froze. That voice. Low, guttural, but familiar. His eyes widened. "Prak?"

The beast's head tilted, golden eyes flashing. "Yeh."

Heartmann's laugh rang out, wild and sharp, as he pushed himself up from the dirt, blood slicking his grin. He twitched once, twice, then leveled his cutlass at the beast.

And just like that, the two monsters squared off.

Atiba lay in the dirt, ribs aching and the buried heart pounding in the soil behind him, as Prak and Heartmann faced each other across the ruin of the clearing.

# CHAPTER 16 - ATIBA

The clearing shook with the weight of monsters.

Prak's beast-form loomed over Atiba, muscles corded, fur bristling, golden eyes blazing with a fury that didn't feel entirely human. Across from him, Heartmann twitched, his grin wide and crimson, cutlass gleaming oily-black in the false light. The two forces collided before Atiba could even drag himself fully upright.

The sound was cataclysm.

Prak slammed into Heartmann like a bullet train, claws raking across his chest, fangs snapping inches from his throat. Heartmann's body jerked with every blow, his bones cracking, flesh tearing… yet he only laughed louder, wild delight spilling into the air like poison. His cutlass swung in brutal arcs, each one ringing against Prak's claws, sparks and shadow bursting with every strike.

Atiba scrambled to his knees, chest burning, barely able to comprehend what he was seeing. His cousin, his cousin!! He fought like a nightmare, and still it wasn't enough to put the madman down.

Then shadows erupted again. Jumbie.

He staggered at first, blood dripping down his temple, his body trembling from exhaustion. But then something shifted. His gaze flicked to Prak—sharp, calculating, almost familiar—and his shoulders squared. Without a word, he lunged.

And suddenly, the rhythm changed.

Prak slashed high, Jumbie struck low. Heartmann reeled, for the first time forced onto the defensive. The two men moved together, their attacks weaving like twin rivers crashing into a stone. Prak's raw, brute force tore gaps open; Jumbie's shadows slithered in to choke and strike through them. One blocked, the other countered. One feinted, the other punished.

It was seamless. Instinctive. Like they'd fought together their entire lives. Atiba's breath caught. He didn't know how, didn't know why, but watching them was like watching gears click into place. Two storms in tandem, fury in harmony.

Heartmann shrieked, his laughter bending into rage. His cutlass spun in a blur, hacking through shadow, slamming against claw. He moved faster, stronger, every twitch of his broken body snapping him back together, his grin splitting wider each time he drew blood.

Prak roared, fangs bared, pressing forward. Jumbie lashed out, shadows clawing across Heartmann's chest. For a heartbeat, the madman faltered. Atiba thought, hoped—they'd done it.

But Heartmann surged back, strength doubling, tripling. He caught Prak's arm mid-swipe, bones cracking beneath his grip, and slammed him into the dirt. Jumbie lunged, but Heartmann's cutlass bit into his shoulder, driving him down to one knee. The madman loomed over both, his face split in a bloody grin, his chest heaving with psychotic glee.

Atiba's pulse hammered. They were losing. Again. And then—ice.

It burst across the ground like a spiky tidal wave, blue-white and blinding, crawling fast up Heartmann's legs before he could move. Frost seized his calves, his thighs, his waist, locking him to the spot in jagged crystalline blocks. He snarled, his body twitching madly as he tried to wrench free.

Esme.

Atiba's head whipped toward her. She was half-collapsed against a tree, her lips cracked and blue, but her hands still outstretched, breath hissing through her teeth. Every shard of her will poured into the ice.

"Now!" she screamed.

Prak moved first. He threw his whole weight onto Heartmann, beast-strength driving the madman down, claws digging into his shoulders. Heartmann thrashed, cutlass swinging wildly, but the ice and the beast's grip pinned him fast.

And Jumbie… Jumbie's shadows surged. His face twisted, rage and something older burning in his eyes. With a roar that shook the trees, he drove his arm forward, shadows hardening around it into a spear. His hand plunged into Heartmann's chest, slicing through ribs, through muscle—deep, deeper, until his entire arm vanished inside.

Heartmann's laughter rose, manic even in agony. "Yes! YES!" Then Jumbie's fist closed. The sound was wet, final.

Heartmann's heart tore free, bursting from his back in a spray of blood and shadow. Jumbie held it high, dripping and writhing in his grip, his chest heaving like a beast that had just torn the world in half.

For the first time, Heartmann's grin faltered. His eyes went wide, his body twitching spasmodically, cutlass slipping from his fingers. He gasped once, twice, then let out a broken laugh that cracked in his throat.

And then he collapsed.

The half-frozen body fell awkwardly, the ice still clutching his legs and hips. His torso twisted unnaturally as it hit the dirt, shards of frost breaking off and scattering across the clearing. The corpse jerked once, twice, then went utterly still, his wide grin frozen in place like a grotesque mask.

The clearing fell silent, save for the echo of their breaths: Prak's, Jumbie's, Esme's, Atiba's all tangled together.

Atiba's chest burned as he stared at the scene before him. His cousin, transformed into something primal and terrifying, and this shadow-born warrior who looked exactly like Levi holding the heart of a monster in his hand.

For the first time since Boisdepin had begun unraveling, Atiba wondered if this was what destiny looked like. Brutal. Bloody. Impossible.

And if he was really meant to stand among it.

# CHAPTER 17 - ESME

sme's chest heaved, her shadows twitching and frayed. She didn't move, didn't defend herself when Prak's glare locked onto her.

He had changed before. She remembered the first time she had seen this transformation, back when he was just a teenager, half-grown, with little control over what boiled in his blood. The shift had ripped through him like a storm, bones cracking, skin stretching, his body reshaping into something older than hunger. Shoulders had widened, knuckles lengthened, his face rearranged until it belonged to a beast.

Lagahoo.

Back then the sight had terrified her. The sound of bones breaking, the way the moon had clung to his new form… Even as "Wail"… it had frozen her where she stood.

Now, though, he moved with control. His beast form loomed before her, immense and dangerous, fur bristling, a muzzle curled back to bare fangs. The terror was still there, prickling at her skin, but guilt pressed heavier.

Even this didn't cancel out the shame that sat like stone in her gut. She had brought this on them in ways she could not undo.

"You." His beast's voice rumbled low, vibrating with fury as he thrust a claw toward the spiked trail of ice leading to Heartmann's mangled body. "Yuh tink you is Darren now?!"

Esme said nothing. The accusation landed like a stone in her chest. The ice—Darren's ice—always left her drained, body and spirit both. She almost never touched it unless forced. The guilt of what she'd taken from its true bearer… and the toll it carved into her with every use… made it a last resort. Her elder brother would have wielded it effortlessly, without the trembling in her bones, without the shame.

Prak's claws flexed, his chest heaving. "You desecrate Boisdepin graves. Nearly kill de boy." He jabbed a claw toward Atiba. "And now you standin' here like you belong?"

Esme lowered her gaze. Her voice, when it came, was quiet, stripped bare. "I don't."

Prak stalked a step closer, golden eyes blazing. "Give me one reason ah shouldn't finish you right now."

Her throat tightened. "Ah doh have one."

The boy's voice cut the space between them. "Stop." They both turned.

Atiba stood pale, shaking, dirt streaked across his face. "I'm not saying I trust her," he said, voice thin but steady. "But if she hadn't frozen him," he gestured at the madman's corpse, "none of us would be standing here."

Prak's claws flexed. His chest rose and fell. And slowly, reluctantly, his beast form receded. The fur shrank back, his claws pulled in, leaving only the man. His bare skin steamed in the cold air, his face hard but human again.

Atiba swallowed, eyes wide. He gazed at Prak, brow furrowed, voice trembling with equal parts fear and demand. "Yeah… about that. What the heck even are you? Are you a werewolf or something?"

Prak's golden eyes, still glowing faintly in the dark, locked on him. His voice came low and rough, still carrying the echo of the beast. "No. Ah Lagahoo."

Atiba blinked, the strange word landing heavy on his tongue. "Laga… what now?"

From the edge of the clearing, the stranger spoke. "Lagahoo. A shapeshifter. A creature who does take on de essence and strengths of beasts." he muttered, his voice rough, impatient. "You to be de nex' Papa Bois an' yuh doh even know dat much?"

Esme's head snapped toward him. Her breath caught. The jawline. The cheekbones. The shadows crawling eagerly to his call. Her throat clenched. "Levi," she whispered, stepping forward before she could stop herself.

Prak turned too. His body stiffened, breath catching in his throat. "Levi…" he whispered, the name breaking out of him before he could stop it. His eyes swept the man's face, every line and shadow, recognition flooding him like a punch to the chest. "Is you. It hadda be you."

The man frowned, shadows curling faintly at his feet. "Ah doh know you," he said flatly. His voice was hard, cautious. "Ah doh know either 'a you."

Prak froze. The words struck harder than any blow, cutting deeper than claw or steel.

"What?" His voice cracked raw, stripped of its usual weight, younger somehow. "Doh play wid me, Levi. You and Darren…" He faltered, chest heaving, memory catching in his throat. "Yuh save meh. Yuh teach meh how to master de transformation when ah couldn't control it. You were mih best friends. Mih bredren. After Darren dead, it was you an' me. We fought together. Side by side."

His hand shook as it lifted, trembling as it pointed at Esme. His golden eyes burned with hurt. "Against she. Against what she bring."

Esme flinched but said nothing.

The silence between them stretched, heavy, until even the forest seemed to lean in. The Levi lookalike's brow furrowed. "Ent ah jus' say ah eh know allyuh?" Shadows rippled at his feet, restless, like they resented the weight of someone else's name.

Prak's hands clenched into fists, his human form trembling with barely contained grief. His voice shook, half-snarl, half-plea. "Den what de hell are you?"

Before either could answer, Atiba finally spoke, his voice hoarse but firm. "Does it matter? Whoever Jumbie is… he helped us. Same as Esme." He turned, jaw tight, eyes lingering on Glo's broken body. "What I want to know is… why? Why would anyone want to hurt her?"

Jumbie's head snapped toward him, shadows flaring like black flame.

"Yuh think Mama D'leau was just a river spirit? No. She was a guardian. A pillar. As Papa Bois watched de forest, she watched de waters. She kept de rivers from bursting dey banks, de seas from swallowing villages whole.

Without she, de waters rage unchecked. Floods, storms, drownings… de price of her absence.”

His voice lowered, heavy with weight. “Papa Bois and Mama D’leau were equals. Two guardians in balance. One guarding root and earth, de other guarding current and tide. Now, within a week, both gone. De stag elusive. De waters still. Dat not coincidence. Somebody clearing de board. Somebody want chaos.”

Atiba swallowed hard, his voice low but steady as he suddenly remembered the madman’s words. “Heartmann said it himself. He said her heart was needed… for some kind of ritual.” He shook his head, the words tasting like ash. “Said that ‘Big man Brown’ needed it.”

The name rippled through the clearing like a chill wind.

Jumbie bristled, shoulders tight, shadows hissing against the dirt.

Prak’s face hardened, realization dawning. He turned sharply to Esme. “So dat was it. Brown trick yuh. Duppy talk. Promise yuh a path to Levi if yuh sacrifice Atiba. All de while, what he really want was Mama D’leau.”

Esme’s lips parted, but no words came. She stared at the ground, shame clinging to her like a shroud.

Prak’s voice dropped low, bitter. “And yuh gave it to him.” Silence pressed heavy.

Jumbie crouched, his movements deliberate, almost reverent. For once, the shadows didn’t bristle or lash out—they sank back, subdued, as his hands pressed into the soil. He worked silently, clawing and shaping the earth into a resting place, his jaw tight, his face unreadable.

Prak stared at him, stunned for a moment. Then, wordlessly, he dropped to his knees beside him. His hands dug into the dirt, his strength carving deeper, faster. Atiba hesitated, but the weight in his chest pulled him down too. Together, the three of them worked: the gruff stranger who looked like Levi, the grandson who had carried Wilberforce's legacy, and the boy still finding his place in all of it.

Esme stood apart. Her hands twitched at her sides, itching to dig, to carry, to do something. She wanted to kneel beside them, to help lay the serpent-woman to rest. But the thought was crushed as quickly as it came. This was her fault. All of it. The madness, the blood, the death. She could almost feel Prak's claws in her throat if she dared suggest she had the right to mourn with them. And Atiba... she had already stolen his trust, his safety, his life once. How could she pretend she belonged in this moment?

So she stayed frozen, watching. Every scrape of earth, every handful of soil piled onto her chest like fresh guilt.

The rhythm of digging became its own kind of prayer. None of them spoke, but the silence was heavy with grief and gratitude. When the grave was ready, Jumbie lifted Glo's body with care, as though she were no heavier than a child. He laid her down gently, his hand lingering for a moment on her slack face. Prak placed her heart in the hollow of her chest before they covered her with earth again. Each handful felt like a promise, of respect, of vengeance, of memory.

Esme pressed a fist to her mouth, her nails digging into her skin, fighting the urge to weep aloud. She had no right.

When it was done, they stood together, breath ragged, hands filthy, the mound of fresh earth gleaming under the Jumbie World's strange sky. And

Esme stayed a step behind, apart, as if the distance itself was the only penance she could still offer.

Silence settled. The kind that pressed down on Esme's shoulders until she could hardly breathe.

Jumbie stood unmoving, his face unreadable. The shadows that once curled like claws at his legs now pooled limp at his feet, subdued, almost grieving. He looked carved from stone, yet tethered by something deeper, something she could not name.

Atiba stood, eyes dropped, shoulders sagging, and a shadow crossing his face deeper than fear. It wasn't just sorrow—she knew sorrow well enough to recognize its weight. This was sharper, rawer, like the ground itself had shifted beneath him.

His gaze fixed on the mound where Mama D'leau's body lay, and he stared as if he could will her back. His face betrayed a storm of conflicting emotions, too tangled for her to name. Esme could only guess at their connection, but whatever it was, he mourned her.

Prak swiped a dirty hand across his brow, streaking soil down his cheek without caring. His chest rose and fell, fury still simmering beneath his skin, but dulled, tempered by the work they had just done.

Then he turned to her, his voice low and sharp. "Dat man. Brown. Who de hell he really is?"

Esme's heart lurched. Of course it would be her. It always came back to her. She had wanted Levi, had been willing to trade anything for him, and Brown had seen it, played her like a fiddle. Her lips parted, then pressed shut. The truth clawed in her chest, refusing to stay hidden.

Finally, she exhaled. "Like I told you in the graveyard. I only met Brown once. He wasn't ordinary. Old, not just in years, but in presence. Like Wilberforce. Like Tanty. He told me Papa Bois stood in the way of tearing down the veil completely. Said the world once lived as one. Human and jumbie side by side. And he wanted that again. No barriers."

Atiba frowned. His voice cracked the stillness. "So Heartmann wasn't just some lone psycho. He was Brown's enforcer."

Esme's throat tightened, but she forced the words out. "Yes. And there's another. A woman calling herself Millicent. She looks harmless and acts like a secretary, but I think she's far more dangerous. Whatever they want, it isn't random. They already know about us. She knew things she shouldn't have, about my abilities, and about both of you... about my past."

Prak spat into the dirt, disgust thick in his voice. "So Brown tryin' a ting. And Mama D'leau was only de first step."

"For a door only her heart could open," Atiba said softly, gesturing to the ground where Heartmann had fallen. "That's what he said."

The words clung to Esme like smoke she could not wash off.

"Dat settles it, ah guess." Jumbie finally straightened. His eyes never left the grave. His voice came quiet but resolute. "Ah eh goin' back with allyuh."

Esme's chest squeezed tight.

Atiba blinked. "What? Why not?"

Jumbie's gaze never left the mound of earth. "Ah doh belong out dere. Dis place is meh tether now. If anyone come for she heart, dey go hadda pass tru me first." Shadows curled tight around his feet again, armor sealing him to the ground.

Atiba started to protest, but Jumbie cut him off. "Ah not even sure ah could exist in de real world now dat she gone. Ah rather not chance it. And besides…" His tone dropped, grim. "Dis man Brown went through all dis trouble to take she heart. Yuh think he go stop here? Nah. He go try again. And again. Somebody need to stay and watch over she."

The words struck Esme like a blade. He didn't know her. Didn't remember her. Didn't even know the name Levi. And yet, here he was, choosing duty, choosing exile, as if he had never been anything else. Her brother had been gone for years, and now this man… this stranger who wore his face, would bury himself beside Mama D'leau without a second thought. It was loyalty she no longer deserved, devotion she could never match. She felt the sting of it like rejection, like grief layered over grief.

Jumbie crouched, pressing a hand gently to the soil, his fingers curling as though to anchor himself forever. "Ah sorry, boss man. Ah had every intention of seein' yuh out, like she asked. But dis…" He nodded at the grave. "Dis more important."

Atiba's throat tightened. For a moment, Esme saw the boy hesitate, saw him wrestle with something too big for words. Then he nodded faintly, his voice low. "I get it."

Prak stared at Jumbie, lips twitching with unspoken argument. But in the end, all he managed was a stiff nod. Esme turned her face away, before any of them could see the tears cutting down her cheeks.

Jumbie stayed kneeling, hand rooted in the dirt, shadows curling up around him like chains he had chosen. He never looked back as the others gathered themselves.

Esme lifted her hand, shadows seeping outward across the dirt like spilled ink. They gathered, rippling until they formed a pool at their feet, black and trembling, alive with the promise of passage.

Atiba froze, breath catching. "No way." His voice cracked, fear raw. "Not again."

Her chest ached at the memory on his face. She had dragged him into the choking dark once already. But this time, her voice stayed steady. "It's the only way. Hold my hand, Atiba. Don't let go. That's all. Just hold on."

Prak stepped forward, his golden eyes blazing. His voice dropped low, every word a threat.

"Esme, if we doh make it through dis together, if you even think about leavin' him behind, den none of we reachin'. Understand?"

Her throat bobbed. She forced herself to meet his gaze and nodded once.

"I understand."

The shadows spread wider, rippling like a living sea. Atiba's hand shook as he slid it into hers. Her fingers were cold, but firm, real. He squeezed, hard enough that it almost hurt, and she let him.

Her eyes flicked to Prak, who gave a sharp nod. She drew in a breath. "On three," she whispered.

They leapt. The shadows surged upward, swallowing them whole.

The weight of the Shadow World gripped Esme's skin, familiar and awful, her curse and her gift. Atiba tensed beside her, but she held fast to his hand, willing her shadows to obey. For a heartbeat, everything was dark. And then… light. Heat. The smell of roasting breadfruit drifting on the night air.

They spilled out onto wooden planks, the veranda of Wilberforce's house.

Esme gasped, releasing Atiba's hand only once she was certain he was steady. Lights flickered down below, laughter drifting up from the village. The world had gone on untouched, as though none of the blood or shadow or grief had happened at all.

And yet Esme knew: nothing was untouched now.

# CHAPTER 18 - ATIBA

The living room of the little house on the hill overlooking Boisdepin was heavy with silence. Atiba sank into his grandfather's armchair, the cushions swallowing him whole. Prak perched on the edge of a chair, stiff-backed and restless, while Esme lingered near the wall of photographs, her arms folded tight, her gaze drifting until it landed on the picture he now knew to be of a younger Darren, Prak, and Levi.

Atiba studied her quietly. She wasn't just mourning her brother, though that was plain in the way her lips pressed together, the faint tremor in her jaw. No, there was more to it.

Esme had once been willing to kill him for the chance to bring Levi back. That kind of desperation didn't come from malice, but from grief sharpened into something dangerous. She had let her loss cloud her judgment, let herself be played by forces bigger than her. And now, seeing Levi alive but hollow, with no memory of her, she must have felt the weight of every terrible choice pressing down on her at once.

Prak's gaze had fixed on the same photo, his whole body coiled tight. Atiba could almost feel what was behind it: the ache of being one of the boys in the frame, the one who had idolized his older friends. Darren and Levi had been his teachers, his protectors, his brothers in all but name. Now Darren was a distant memory, and Levi had seemingly returned to the world again, but stripped of all their shared history. For Prak, it must have felt like losing him twice.

Jumbie. Levi. Whoever he truly was.

Atiba cleared his throat. The sound scraped against the stillness. "Alright. Enough. I need to know." His eyes cut between them. "What's the real history between you two? Between you and Levi? I'm tired of being the only one left in the dark."

Prak's jaw tightened. His fingers flexed once, then eased. "Leh she explain."

Esme turned slowly. Her arms dropped to her sides. For a heartbeat Atiba thought she'd refuse, but then she spoke. "Very well."

"This is the story as it was passed down in my family." Her voice was calm, deliberate. "Long ago, back in colonial Trinidad, a French planter came to the island seeking his fortune. He wanted wealth and high society, but no matter what he tried, he could never gain it… until a slave woman, a strong obeah woman, fell in love with him."

Atiba frowned. "Obeah? What's that?"

Esme glanced at him. "A practice. Older than this island's sugar, older than its churches. Power drawn from spirits, rituals, herbs, sacrifice. People call it witchcraft, some say it's like voodoo. But it's more… willpower bent into the marrow of the world."

Atiba swallowed. That single word—sacrifice—stuck.

Esme continued. "He used her gifts to rise in society. And once she secured him the influence he craved, he discarded her for the daughter of a wealthy plantation owner."

Prak cleared his throat and shifted where he sat, unease flickering across his face at the thought of a woman used and then cast aside.

"She did not take that lightly," Esme said flatly, her gaze fixed on some point far beyond the wall of photographs. "She cursed him. Not just him, but his children. She reached into the Jumbie World itself, something no ordinary woman should have been able to do, and pulled a piece of it into her hands. She bound that essence, raw and violent, into his bloodline like a brand."

Her voice grew quieter, steadier, almost clinical as she explained, though the tension in her shoulders betrayed her. "From then on, every time three siblings were born to a Porter, the curse woke. Their blood carried power, unnatural and volatile. One might command the elements. Another might warp the body. Another might bend the will of others. It was never the same twice, but it was always destructive. The curse made them extraordinary... and it made them rivals."

Atiba shifted uneasily in his grandfather's chair. "Wait," he said, his words stumbling out, "so... they were just doomed? From the start? No matter what?" His voice cracked with disbelief.

Esme's eyes flicked to him, but she didn't answer right away.

"That's how you got yours, isn't it?" Atiba pressed, realization dawning slowly. "That's why you can... do what you do. The curse."

Esme's eyes flicked to him, cool but not unkind. "Yes. That is how Darren, Levi, and I got ours. Darren was the eldest, and his gift was cryokinesis: the ability to create and control ice. He could freeze a pond solid in seconds, or draw blades of frost straight from the air."

Her lips tightened faintly, a mix of sorrow and admiration. "Levi's was shadows. He could bend them, shape them, make them tangible. Bind, suffocate, even cut with them. He could even travel in between shadows to places he had already been as long as there was a shadow at the other end. His was… the strongest, I believe."

She paused before continuing, her voice low. "Mine was my voice. A siren's voice. With it, I could slip into someone's mind and bend their will… make them see me as friend, lover, savior. It doesn't work on everyone, but most…" She trailed off, then forced herself to finish. "Most are easy."

Atiba blinked, the memory snapped into place. The graveyard. Her eyes fixed on him, her voice as casual as if she'd told him the time. "Stop breathing." He hadn't understood then why she would say something so strange, so cruel. And when nothing happened, he had written it off as some twisted joke. But now, hearing her confess, the truth hit him like a blow.

She had been testing her power on him, seeing if her voice could bend him too.

Relief stirred in him, sharp and quiet. It hadn't worked. He was glad of that—yet even as the thought settled, another pressed close behind. Why hadn't it? Some part of him, the part tied to the forest and the stag's burning gaze, whispered that the answer lay deeper than chance.

His reaction flickered across his face before he could hide it, and he knew she saw it. She clocked it, but didn't acknowledge.

Her fingers curled at her side as she continued. "The true cruelty of it was that the curse didn't only gift power, it poisoned the family's bond. It whispered that one sibling could take another's strength. That blood could be consumed by blood. And so, again and again, they destroyed each other to claim more. Brother against brother. Sister against sister. Whole branches of the family tree burned down to ash because the curse demanded it."

"When Darren died," she continued, her tone flat but steady, "the curse answered. His ice spread to both Levi and myself. And when Levi fell, his fraction of Darren's power, as well as his own shadow ability, both became mine."

She exhaled, sharp and tired. "That was the legacy she left behind. Not a blessing, not a warning, but a cycle of power and slaughter written into their very veins."

She stepped away from the photographs, her voice steady and clipped, like she had rehearsed this before. "Derwin Porter, the current Prime Minister of Trinidad and Tobago, carried that same blood. Darren was his eldest, legitimate son; I was the second, his illegitimate daughter born of an affair he never acknowledged; and Levi was the third child. We were the cursed trio. The curse isn't some distant legend. It's our family. Our lives."

Atiba swallowed hard, the weight of it landing with new clarity.

Esme continued. "I may be a Porter, but I am also descended from her, the obeah woman. The one who cursed the Frenchman and his sons. Her name… we knew her only as Tanty."

Atiba blinked. "You knew her?"

"Yes. She was powerful. She simply refused to die. She stretched her life with rituals until there was little left but a husk of flesh and bone. For generations, she manipulated her descendants, grooming women to serve her cause. And when her strength waned too far to sustain her, she sought another way. A legacy."

Her eyes darkened. "That was me. Her final design. She orchestrated my birth. She made sure my mother, her own great-great-great-granddaughter, found Derwin Porter and seduced him. Not that it was difficult." A flicker of venom twisted her mouth. "He was never the choosy type."

The bitterness passed, her voice steadying again. "So I became both: heir to her bloodline, and bastard child of the Porter line."

Atiba's stomach knotted. "So you were made to be…"

"The bridge," Esme said flatly. "The key. The way to regain the last vestige of her once massive power: the Porter curse. When Levi was born, with Darren already older, the curse stirred awake. Three siblings again.

"And Tanty made certain I was bound to them. She wouldn't be forgotten; she wanted her wound to outlive the men who made it."

She moved from the wall, standing straighter now, her voice stronger.

"I was raised to believe this was destiny. That the Porter family deserved punishment. That their blood had always been tainted by greed and betrayal. And that I would be the vessel to carry it through. Groomed since birth to inherit all three gifts."

Prak muttered under his breath. "Tanty poison yuh mind."

Esme ignored him. "I trained. I learned to use my voice, the siren's gift. But I knew one day, it would not be enough. I would need theirs. So when I was grown, I found Darren. He was married then, with children. But also searching for a psychologist."

Atiba blinked. "You?"

"Yes." Esme's mouth tightened. "He had questions. Concerns about Levi. He wanted help for his younger brother. And I... offered it. Slipped into their lives as a professional, all the while wearing that white, featureless mask and my alter ego—Wail—like a second skin. As Wail, I started a gang, used my voice to gather men to serve me. I tested myself against other criminal elements... And as Esme, I earned Darren's trust."

Atiba tilted his head. "Your... alter ego?" he asked, tilting his head. "What do you mean by that?"

Esme blinked, pulled out of the memory for a moment. "Wail was what they called me," she said. "I created her as a way to test myself and my powers in real life. I wanted a version of me that could move freely, amass the resources I needed to carry out Tanty's plans. Esme couldn't do that in the open. Wail could. I had a mask made, and when I put it on, I was her."

She lifted one shoulder, almost sheepish. "As Wail, I could push my voice, see what it could do, lead men, take territory. Esme had limitations. Wail didn't."

Atiba watched her. "Why 'Wail'?" he asked. "Why that name?"

A tiny, almost embarrassed smile flickered over her face. Her eyes dropped for half a heartbeat before she looked back up. "It wasn't the most creative choice," she admitted. "But my power is my voice. People heard me before they saw me. Sometimes it was a cry in the dark, sometimes it was a command. It fit. And… it sounded like mourning. Which was what I was doing, even then."

She let that hang a moment, then her tone settled again as she slipped back into the story, like the pause had never happened.

She continued, her voice dropping. "I cared for Darren. More than I was supposed to. Which is why I did not… I could not strike him myself." Esme broke eye contact. "I had my own men kill him when the time came. With his powers he could have easily taken them but… he thought I was in trouble. He came running to my rescue. Into an ambush. Even now…" Her throat caught. "Even now, I feel that weight."

Atiba's hands curled into fists on the armrest. "And Levi?"

Her expression softened, conflicted. "Levi was different. My voice had no sway over him. Perhaps because of what he was. Perhaps because his mind was… closed to it." She glanced at Prak. "But the more I worked with him, the more I grew to care for him too. In a way I didn't expect. Like a kid brother. As Esme, I wanted to shield him. As Wail… I was bound to destroy him."

Atiba struggled to keep up, brow furrowed. "Wait a sec… back up a bit. Why did Darren need a psychologist for Levi?"

Prak scoffed. "Because… de guy was literally a psychopath."

Esme's voice sharpened instantly.

"No. He was a high-functioning sociopath. There is a distinction. He had a void where emotion should have been. Darren taught him how to react, taught him what mask to wear for any given situation. With Darren gone…

Levi was left with no one to hold him, to control his base impulses… to force him into being normal. And so he let go. The way he fought. The way he thought. Brilliant. Cold. Untouchable.”

Atiba’s stomach knotted. The thought of someone like Jumbie wielding that kind of power with no conscience behind it made his skin crawl.

Prak leaned forward, elbows on his knees, shoulders hunched. “One ah dey father’s outside women curse him when he was small. A spiteful ting. She try to twist de boy wid obeah. But it couldn’t tek hold proper… de Porter curse already inside him, stronger, older. It clash and fail, but it still leave a scar.” He tapped his chest. “Tek away all he feelings. Leave him hollow.” His eyes darkened. “Levi was dangerous. Dangerous, but…”

His expression softened, gaze shifting toward the photo wall. His voice dropped, quieter now. “He was good too. He protect de people he care about. Save me more than once. Whatever was missing in him, he still fight to be more than dat.”

Esme’s eyes flicked from Atiba to Prak, a faint spark softening her otherwise stern expression. “That was Levi… and Darren, I suppose, to a T. Always shielding others. Always stepping in. Getting close to them… it made me question things I had never dared before. The stories I was raised on, the destiny Tanty had drilled into me. For a time, I almost believed I could step away from it all, that I could be something different.”

She lowered her eyes, her voice quieting. “But even closeness could not stop Tanty’s demands. The old woman pressed me harder, pushed me to finish what had been set in motion long before I was born. I thought I could stall her, delay the inevitable. But she was relentless. She told me Levi had to die, just like Darren. That only then would the curse reach its fulfillment. The only way our legacy could be secured."

Prak's jaw worked, his voice sharp. "So yuh betray him."

She glanced up, defensive at first, then resigned. "I set the trap. I kidnapped Prak, used him as bait. I thought Levi would come because of loyalty, or guilt, or something human. But when he appeared…" Her mouth curved faintly, bitter. "He told me he had only come because I had insulted him. That I had taken something of his. That was enough."

Prak gave a short, humorless laugh, remembering.

"He wasn't wrong."

Atiba shifted uneasily in his grandfather's chair, the image of this cold, brilliant Levi sharpening in his mind.

"And then what?"

Esme's hands clenched into fists. "He tore through my men. Cut them down like they were nothing. Then I forced Prak to fight him. Levi weakened. I drove the knife into him myself." Her voice cracked, but she pressed on. "And in that moment, something shattered."

The room was very still. Atiba leaned forward, caught in the weight of her words. "The Day of Darkness."

"Yes." Esme's voice was flat, though her eyes glistened. "The stab wound was fatal, but he slipped into the shadows to die. When he did, the weaker curse that had clung to him all those years finally broke. His emotions, years upon years of silence, erupted all at once. Rage, grief, love, fear. It tore through the world, pulled shadows into the living. Prak's tone was low, steady. "We thought it only cover de warehouse we was in, but…"

Esme's gaze fell. "Levi covered the entire island in an instant."

Atiba hadn't been in Trinidad then, but the weight of it pressed on him all the same. A shadow left behind, and somehow, it felt like his to carry now.

"In that storm, Tanty revealed her plan," the woman continued, "She meant to take my body for her own, to live again through me. My aunts, my cousins… they held me down as she prepared the ritual. But Levi… even dying, even drowning in all that chaos, he saved me. His shadows wrapped me, hardened over me. For a moment, we shared one mind, one breath. He forgave me then. Told me we were pawns in a game older than either of us."

Her throat tightened. "And in those last moments, using the shadows he'd covered me with, he took control of me… of my body. He used my hands, my strength, my will, and with them, he ended her. Tanty's centuries-long grip, gone in an instant. Burned out by the very bloodline she had tried to curse into monsters."

Her voice cracked for the first time. "He didn't blame me. That forgiveness… it burned worse than any curse."

The silence pressed heavy over the room. Even Prak, arms folded across his chest and his scowl set like stone, said nothing at first.

Then he exhaled, sharp through his nose. "It was only after all dat we really understand wha' happen," he muttered. "Grandpa feel it de moment it start, but by de time he reach, it was too late. Draggin' dat whole shadow-realm into de real world… dat was de first lil tear in de veil. Even Grandpa couldn' stitch it back. De only ting we could do was keep de worse creatures dat slip through from mashin' up everyting."

His gaze shifted toward Esme, hard and steady. "Ah not forgiving yuh. Not now. Maybe not ever. But…" His throat tightened; the words came rough. "If Levi could, maybe one day ah could too. But doh hold yuh breath."

Esme inclined her head, her voice low, solemn. "Fair."

Atiba sat back, heart pounding, trying to take it all in. A cursed bloodline. A centuries-old witch. A brother who tore the world apart in death. His own cousin caught in the middle. And Esme, standing there, admitting it all, looking smaller than he had ever seen her.

"Then…" Atiba's voice was careful. "Where does that leave us now?"

Esme didn't answer. Her arms wrapped tighter around herself, as though she could squeeze back the years of guilt pressing in.

Prak sighed and rose to his feet. "Now… we prepare. Whatever Brown plannin', it big. Bigger than we. An' if we go stop him, Atiba…" His voice dropped, steady but rough. "Yuh need to wake up. Become Papa Bois proper, like grandpa thought you could."

Atiba's chest tightened, the words slamming into him harder than he expected. He had wondered, quietly, if his grandfather had meant for him to be anything more than a caretaker of the house, a reluctant heir to land and memory. But this… this was different. This was a legacy. Responsibility.

Wilberforce had chosen him.

Prak's eyes held his, unwavering. "But listen good: it eh go be easy. With Grandpa gone, de veil thin, de balance shake. De forces movin' now?

Dangerous. More dangerous dan you could even picture. Dat madman we fight in de Jumbie World… Heartmann? Da'is jus' a taste of what comin'. So really tink it through. Doh step into dis halfway."

He leaned back slightly, though his gaze never wavered. "But if yuh ready. If yuh decide to take de mantle. Ah wid yuh. Same way Grandpa woulda been."

Esme's voice softened unexpectedly. "I'll help too. Whatever it takes. If you'll have me… And…" her eyes on Atiba, glimmering faintly, "I am sorry. For everything."

Atiba studied her for a long moment. He saw no guile in her now…no 'Wail,' no deceit. Just a woman hollowed out by mistakes she couldn't undo. "I forgive you," he said finally. Simply.

Her breath caught, like she hadn't expected him to say it.

Silence settled over the trio again, heavy as a shroud. The weight of all they had shared hung between them, unspoken but inescapable. At last, Esme's voice cut through, low and uncertain. "So… what now?"

He leaned back in Wilberforce's chair, rubbing his face. "I don't know what I need yet," he admitted. His voice dropped. "Right now, I guess… just time to think."

After a long moment, Atiba rose. The weight of the chair and the house pressed too heavily on his shoulders. He crossed to the guestroom, shut the door behind him, and lay down.

# CHAPTER 19 - ATIBA

Atiba woke to the sound of two roosters crowing somewhere in the distance. The cries overlapped, sharp and insistent, breaking apart the last scraps of restless dreams. His body felt heavy, his mind raw. He had tossed and turned for hours, images tearing through him no matter how tightly he shut his eyes. Mama D'leau—Glo—her face glowing with kindness before it faded into still water. Heartmann's twisted grin, the shadows curling from Jumbie's hands, Esme's guilt, Prak's fury. It all pressed into him until exhaustion had finally dragged him under.

And all this in less than a week.

He pressed the heel of his hand against his eyes. He had come to Trinidad for a funeral. Instead, he had found himself drowning in curses, jumbies, and guardians. It felt absurd. Impossible. Yet here he was, still breathing, and none of it had been a dream.

The guestroom was dim, dawn only beginning to creep through the slats of the window. He dressed slowly, pulling on a clean shirt and jeans. At the door, his eyes caught the faint chalky line of salt across the threshold. He frowned. He'd swept it all away when he cleaned the house days ago. But last night, after the heavy talk with Esme and Prak, the line had been back, Prak's doing. Salt keeps de jumbies out. *Doh play foolish, 'Tiba.*

Atiba hesitated, then stepped carefully over it. If the world really was as strange and dangerous as he now knew, maybe a little salt wasn't the worst precaution.

The house was quiet. No Prak. No Esme. He was alone. And that felt both lighter and heavier at once. He needed air.

Outside, Boisdepin was waking. Smoke curled up from cookfires, carrying the smell of frying bakes and cocoa tea. Radios crackled with morning news. The world here woke slowly, without rush, like the sun itself. Another rooster crowed late, as if reluctant to admit the day had started at all.

His feet, unthinking, carried him to the hill where the old cemetery lay.

The gate creaked sharp against the hush, as if reluctant to open for him. Bougainvillea spilled red and purple across the fence, fighting the gray of stone. He found the mound easily, the simple marker carved with his grandfather's name.

Wilberforce DuBois.

Atiba crouched low, pressing his palms into the dirt. "I don't even know where to start, Pops."

The words spilled sharp and fast, about the funeral, about Boisdepin pulling him under, about jumbies and guardians and the weight everyone seemed to expect him to carry. "You were steady, Pops. Carved from stone, they say. And me? I'm just a guy from Queens. Why me? Why not Prak?"

Silence pressed heavy, but he kept going. "But Glo believed in me. And that stag keeps showing up like it's waiting. And I can't shake the way Boisdepin feels when I walk through it. Like the ground itself won't let me go."

His throat burned. "I don't want to fail. Not them. Not this place. Not you."

As the words left him, raw and trembling, the wooden bangle at his wrist stirred with a faint glow. It pulsed once, warm and steady, like a hand resting on his shoulder, like Wilberforce himself… no… Papa Bois… saying without words that he wasn't alone. Atiba stared at it, breath catching, the ache in his chest loosening.

He bowed his head once toward the grave. "Thanks, Pops. See you later." From the cemetery, his feet carried him down the winding road. The sun had climbed higher, heat pressing on his back as the path sloped toward the coast. Soon the sea spread wide before him, blinding with light, the horizon endless. He stood in the surf for a long while, letting the salt wind clear his head. For a moment, the madness of the past days felt far away.

But when the heat grew too much, hunger pressed in. His stomach twisted, reminding him he hadn't eaten since that bake and saltfish yesterday.

Almost without thinking, his feet took him back toward the village, right back toward Barbra's shop.

The young woman looked up as Atiba pushed the door open, the bell above it chiming softly. She was bent over a basket of fresh bread, hands dusted with flour, her curls pulled back in a loose knot. When she saw him, her whole face brightened in that easy way of hers, like the morning had been waiting on him to arrive.

"Well, look who de cat drag in," she teased, her voice lilting. "Morning, Atiba. Yuh eat yet?"

"Good morning."

He shifted awkwardly in the doorway.

"No. Not yet."

"Eh-eh, man."

She clicked her tongue, already reaching for a knife.

"Cyah start yuh day like dat."

Before he could argue, she was moving—slicing bread, cracking eggs into a pan, the sharp hiss of oil filling the space. Atiba leaned against the counter, the warmth and smell of frying tomatoes wrapping around him.

A few minutes later, she slid a plate toward him, a sandwich stacked high, still steaming, and set down a mug of coffee dark enough to wake the dead. "Eat," she said simply, her tone gentle but firm, more command than suggestion.

He didn't resist. The first bite burst warm against his tongue, yolk bleeding golden down the bread. Comforting, grounding. "Thanks," he murmured, meaning it more than he expected.

Barbra leaned on the counter, chin resting on her hand. Her gaze was steady, not prying but open, waiting.

"Something bothering yuh," she said softly. Not a question.

Atiba froze mid-bite. He swallowed. "I've got a choice to make," he admitted. "Feels… impossible."

Her head tilted as she studied him. Then her smile returned, small but sure. "Impossible, hm? Or just heavy?"

He met her eyes, startled by the calm in her tone.

"People who honest," she went on, "people who steady, like you… dey does find de right way more often than not. I doh know what yuh carrying, but I believe you go make de right choice."

Her words sank deep. She didn't know the half of what weighed on him, yet her faith landed like an anchor on shifting ground. He found himself watching her longer than he meant to, the way the morning light caught her curls, the curve of her smile, the ease with which she leaned into his heaviness. Something stirred in him, quiet and unexpected.

"Thank you," he said at last, voice rougher than he intended.

Barbra shrugged, though her eyes softened. "You seem like de kind of man people could trust. De kind who eh afraid to stand when it count. Dat alone does set yuh apart." Her gaze lingered, thoughtful. "Wilberforce was like dat too. Quiet most times, but steady. When he plant heself, nothing could move him. I see a little 'a dat in you."

For a moment the silence stretched between them, warm instead of heavy. Atiba sipped his coffee, suddenly sure he wanted to come back here tomorrow, if only to see her smile like that again.

"High. Low. Jack. Game!" A round of groans and laughter erupted from the back of the shop.

Atiba glanced over. Donny sat like a king at his table, cards fanned in hand, three younger men squirming under his grin. The slap of cards and the rhythm of banter filled the room, thick as the scent of frying food.

Barbra caught Atiba watching. "All Fours," she explained with a smile. "Card game. Big ting down here. Daddy doh lose often."

"Looks serious."

"Serious enough."

As if summoned, Donny's eyes snapped to him.

"Boy, yuh know how to play?"

Atiba blinked.

"Uh… no, sir."

"Good. Time to learn."

Atiba hesitated, but Donny's stare left no room for refusal. He sighed and slid into the chair.

The game swept him up fast—slapping cards, shouting points, Donny barking corrections at him, the younger men ribbing him mercilessly. Atiba fumbled at first, but by the second round, the rhythm hooked him. By the third, he was laughing with them, the city weight loosening from his shoulders.

When Donny finally partnered with him, the old man leaned close, muttering quick strategy. Together, they crushed the table. The young men groaned; Donny just grinned and clapped Atiba's back hard enough to sting. "Not bad, city boy. Yuh might learn yet."

Atiba grinned back, flushed, realizing he was enjoying himself… really enjoying himself. Not as an outsider, but as part of it. The chatter, the teasing, the easy warmth of being among people who claimed him without asking.

From the counter, Barbra watched, arms folded, her smile soft, almost proud. Every time his eyes found hers, something unspoken lingered there, warm enough to make him stumble over his next play.

She caught the slip, the corner of her mouth curving as if she knew exactly why he'd fumbled. When the laughter at the table eased and the players decided they'd taken enough of a beating from Donny, she leaned closer across the counter.

"So," she said quietly, just for him. "When yuh leaving, Atiba?"

The question hit harder than he expected. His stomach dipped, the noise of the shop dulling around him. For a second he almost wished he could pretend he hadn't heard. But the truth pressed in.

He looked up, throat tight. "Day after next." Too soon.

Her smile faltered, just for a heartbeat, before she caught it again. But her eyes lingered on him, softer, vulnerable.

"Well… ah go miss yuh." The words were simple, but they landed heavier than he expected, like truth slipped out before she could dress it in anything lighter.

Then her lips quirked, mischief sparking back to the surface. "Maybe ah should cook some cascadura fuh yuh before yuh leave."

His brows rose. "Cascadura?"

She laughed softly at his confusion. "It's a little freshwater fish. Real bony, but sweet if yuh cook it right. Old legend say, anyone who eat cascadura, no matter where in de world they wander, they does always end up back here. Back in Trinidad to finish dey days."

Atiba blinked, trying to gauge if she was joking. But her eyes held that playful glint, layered with something deeper.

"Da'is the legend, anyways," she finished, turning back to the counter. "So maybe ah feed yuh cascadura, and then ah know fuh sure yuh go come back."

The thought lingered with him long after the cards were cleared.

When the shop finally quieted, Barbra disappeared into the kitchen and returned with a warm paper bag, holding it out with both hands. "Dinner. For you and Prak. Doh let him say ah starve yuh."

Atiba accepted it, the heat seeping through to his palms. "Thanks," he murmured, meaning it more than he expected.

Her fingers brushed his just briefly, her smile softening again. Then she turned back to the counter, leaving him with the bag and the weight of her words echoing in his chest.

Outside, evening settled soft over Boisdepin. The sea breeze moved gently around him, and he felt less like a stranger, more like he was exactly where he was meant to be.

When he reached the veranda, night had fallen cool and quiet. Children chased fireflies, a radio hummed soca in the distance, and the rhythm of life went on untouched by shadows or curses. The paper bag still warm in his hand and the memory of Barbra's words steady in his chest brought him a sense of calm he'd never have thought he'd manage when he woke up that morning. Her quiet faith in him echoed the same weight he'd felt at his grandfather's grave, as if Barbra and Wilberforce both were reminding him that he wasn't standing alone. Boisdepin called to him—not just the house, not just the family name, but the soil itself.

His thoughts churned. He remembered the stag at the funeral, its gaze burning through him like fire.

Glo, who had seemed so humble, so kind, and yet had stood equal to Papa Bois himself, trusting him even when he hadn't trusted himself. Prak, sharp-edged but unyielding, pushing him forward despite being passed over.

Esme, hollowed by guilt, but still choosing to fight. And Levi… Jumbie… whatever he had become, still guarding the broken line between worlds.

Atiba's jaw tightened. He thought of New York, the noise, the anonymity, the comfort of knowing who he was there. Just another guy. Life there was safe. Predictable. Small.

But life here? Life here was messy, heavy, terrifying. And alive in a way he couldn't turn from.

His gaze dropped to the wooden bangle on his wrist. Wilberforce's last gift, pressed into his hand at the funeral. A plain circle of wood, carved smooth and worn with years, yet heavy with meaning. It wasn't just a keepsake. It was a charge. A reminder that blood alone didn't make him Papa Bois. Choice did.

Wilberforce had carried it with certainty, as if he never doubted where he stood. Atiba carried it with hesitation, every step forward shadowed by doubt. But even so, the bangle's weight was steady on his wrist, as if whispering that strength didn't mean never wavering. It meant standing anyway.

The way villagers spoke of Wilberforce's steadiness, the reverence in their eyes when they called his name. The certainty that he had carried something larger than himself and never faltered beneath it. That belief clung to the bangle now, not as a crushing weight, but as proof that someone before him had borne it and that maybe, just maybe, he could too.

Then movement caught his eye.

There, just beyond the fence line where the yard melted into shadow, stood the stag. Tall, luminous, proud, its antlers branching wide like a crown of living wood. It didn't move toward him this time. It only stood, silent, watching.

The sight stole the breath from his chest. The same stag that had marked Wilberforce once, that had stood in quiet reverence at the old man's funeral. And now, here it was again. Not demanding. Not pressing. Just waiting. As if to say: the choice is still yours.

Atiba's hand tightened on the bangle. Green light flared from deep within the grain of its wood, like dawn breaking through a shuttered window, brighter than it had ever been, steady and unshaken. It pulsed in rhythm with his heartbeat, answering the stag's gaze. His chest steadied. The doubt that had gnawed at him for days felt quieter now, pressed beneath something harder, truer. Conviction.

The thought made his chest ache, heavy and clear all at once. Almost without realizing, he reached for his phone. The glowing screen lit his face in pale light as he brushed his thumb over the curve of the bangle like it might lend him its strength. And he pressed call.

It rang once. Twice. Three times. "Hello?"

His mother's voice, distant but sharp as ever, cut through the line. "Hey, Ma." His throat tightened, but the words came steady. "I'm not selling the house. I'm staying in Trinidad."

# EPILOGUE

The lantern hissed in the damp night, its flame flickering against the press of the bush. Every insect seemed to have stilled, the forest too quiet, as if the very air was holding its breath.

Ms. Millicent adjusted her blazer, brushing a stray bit of leaf from her lapel. The red earth clung to everything here—clothes, shoes, lungs. She despised it. A woman like her belonged in climate-controlled offices, beneath the glow of recessed lighting, not here where the smell of mud and stagnant water clung like mildew.

But business did not care for comfort. And tonight, business was a ritual. The crossroads stretched out beneath the canopy, four narrow bush roads cutting into the dark like scars. At the center, a rusting zinc basin had been dragged into place, its sides dented, its belly half-filled with water gone murky from herbs and coins.

Inside, a young man crouched, his knees drawn tight to his chest. Thin shoulders, twitching hands, skin slick with sweat. His eyes darted from the basin to the trees to Millicent herself, desperate for an anchor. He looked like someone waiting for a sentence he didn't understand.

Circling him was the obeahman. The old priest's bare feet whispered against the dirt, moving in deliberate arcs. He trailed smoke and powders in his wake, handfuls of leaves and roots tossed into the basin with each pass. His mutters rode the air like insects, too soft to catch but too sharp to ignore.

With every word, the shadows around the crossroads thickened, leaning inward, as though listening.

Millicent clicked her tongue.

"How much longer?"

"Patience," the obeahman rasped, his eyes fixed on the boy.

"Patience," Millicent echoed dryly, her eyes narrowing. "Patience doesn't pay dividends."

The boy flinched at her voice, his lip trembling. "Miss… I—I don't know if I can do this. Maybe… maybe I not ready."

Her gaze turned on him, flat as polished stone. "You agreed. That makes you ready."

He swallowed, knuckles whitening where he clutched the basin's rim. "But if… if it wrong—"

"Quiet," the obeahman snapped, his cracked voice suddenly sharp. The leaves at his feet shivered, though no wind stirred.

Millicent's stare lingered on the boy a moment longer. Her expression betrayed nothing, no sympathy, no disdain. Only calculation. "Stay in the basin. Don't embarrass yourself."

The air thickened. The herbs hissed as they sank. Coins clinked dully against the metal. The obeahman's mutters deepened, his voice building into something that was not language anymore but force. The basin rattled against the earth. The water began to ripple.

The boy whimpered, pressing himself back, his eyes wide. "Miss—Miss, something movin' in de water—"

"Then stop looking at it," Millicent said briskly.

The priest's voice rose, cracked, then split into a shriek that wasn't wholly human. The shadows pulled tighter, wrapping the crossroads in a curtain of dark. A smell curled out from the basin—sulfur, blood, and wet iron. The water frothed, black against black, hissing as though it boiled.

The boy seized the basin's rim with both hands, his body jerking. His head snapped back, mouth open in a soundless scream. For a moment his chest convulsed, ribs heaving as if something inside were clawing its way out. A thin line of blood slipped from his ear and kept going, drawing itself into the basin like a thread.

Then stillness.

The water went quiet. The air fell dead.

Slowly, the boy lifted his head. When his eyes opened, they burned—not bright, but fever-red, the glow of embers choking for air.

Millicent stepped forward, heels sinking slightly into the soft soil. She studied him with the dispassion of an auditor inspecting a balance sheet. His trembling had stopped. His shoulders squared. A grin pulled across his face, wider than before, too wide for comfort.

"Well," Millicent said crisply. She closed her portfolio with a neat snap. "That's finished, then."

The boy, no longer meek, let out a laugh. At first it cracked like dry wood, low and hesitant. Then it grew, sharp and jagged, bubbling at the edges until it carried a feverish pitch. It echoed down the roads, the sound of glass dragged across stone.

Millicent didn't blink. She inclined her head. "Another Heartmann."

The laugh rose higher, tipping into the familiar, manic, shrill, the sound of hunger that could never be fed. His grin split wider, his fingers twitching like claws eager for something soft to crush.

The shadows at the crossroads leaned closer, listening. The Heartmann was back.

The boy's laughter rattled the trees, shrill and giddy, scattering the night birds from their roosts. The sound twisted in the air until it was almost the same as before.

Almost.

Millicent did not flinch. She stepped closer, her heels finding purchase in the soft dirt, and with a snap of her fingers, her driver emerged from the shadows carrying a long garment bag. She unzipped it with the precision of a surgeon, revealing the gleam of a suit—tailored, expensive, cut in cream with a blood-red tie and a silk square at the breast pocket.

She held it out as though she were handing over a uniform. "Every Heartmann needs his attire," she said simply.

The boy's grin faltered only long enough for him to reach out, his hands trembling with eagerness. He ran his fingers across the fabric, reverent, then clutched it to his chest as if it were a second skin. His laughter bubbled up again, higher this time, edges frayed with mania.

Millicent's expression hardened. "Enough. Your predecessor's mishandling of the D'leau account has already cost us dearly. We missed a deadline because of his… indulgence." Her voice was clipped, businesslike, each word precise as a ledger line. "That cannot happen again. We must fix it—and quickly."

The boy only grinned wider, teeth too sharp in the half-light. He said nothing, just cradled the suit as if it were already stitched to his bones.

"Good," Millicent said briskly. "Then we understand each other."

She turned without ceremony, her heels clicking against the dirt path as she walked back into the bush road from which she had come. The newly minted Heartmann followed, still grinning, still silent.

Her driver was already waiting at the edge of the bush road, engine humming low. The black sedan's headlights cut thin beams through the trees. Millicent slid into the back without breaking stride, the new Heartmann climbing in after her, still clutching his suit like a prize.

The door shut with a heavy thud. The driver shifted into gear. Gravel crunched under the tires as the car pulled onto the narrow road, shadows chasing in its wake.

For a moment, only the sound of tires and the boy's faint, manic laughter filled the night. Then the rear lights flared, catching on the mud-streaked plate: 333.

The number burned in the dark like an omen, a signature as unmistakable as the hunger still echoing in the boy's laugh.

The car disappeared into the bush, carrying Ms. Millicent and her Heartmann toward whatever came next.